"Show me what you've got, city slicker."

Ben glanced back as he hauled himself into the pickup bed. Why did Marley have to look so gorgeous? He shouldn't even be here, at her mission, much less succumbing to an attraction with no future.

Marley cocked her head. "You gonna stay up there all day?" Her smile faded. "I understand, really, if volunteering isn't your thing—"

"Not at all," he said. Then he grabbed one of the boxes.

After they'd unloaded all the supplies and sat sipping cold sodas, Ben couldn't resist glancing at her.

Don't mess with Marley.

Her coworker's subtle warning shouldn't bother him. He had no intention of letting anything develop between him and Marley. Yeah, there was something special about her.

But he had no intention of staying.

He should make some excuse and get out of here. Cut and run right now.

His mind was made up...so why couldn't he move?

Award-winning author **Myra Johnson** writes emotionally gripping stories about love, life and faith. She is a two-time finalist for the ACFW Carol Award and winner of the 2005 RWA Golden Heart. Married since 1972, Myra and her husband have two married daughters and seven grandchildren. Although Myra is a native Texan, she and her husband now reside in North Carolina, sharing their home with two pampered rescue dogs.

Books by Myra Johnson

Love Inspired

Rancher for the Holidays

Visit the Author Profile page at Harlequin.com for more titles.

Rancher for
the Holidays

Myra Johnson

HARLEQUIN® LOVE INSPIRED®

LOVE INSPIRED BOOKS

Recycling programs
for this product may
not exist in your area.

ISBN-13: 978-0-373-81875-4

Rancher for the Holidays

Printed in U.S.A.

Love must be sincere. Hate what is evil; cling to what is good. Be devoted to one another in love. Honor one another above yourselves. Never be lacking in zeal, but keep your spiritual fervor, serving the Lord. Be joyful in hope, patient in affliction, faithful in prayer. Share with the Lord's people who are in need. Practice hospitality.

—*Romans* 12:9–13

For my amazing agent and cherished friend,
Natasha Kern, who never gives up on a good story.

Acknowledgments

I'm sincerely grateful, first of all,
to my longtime friend Peggy Gallagher Fisher,
who mentioned in a Christmas letter one year
that she thought the real town of Candelaria,
Texas, could be a great basis for one of my novels.
Through a series of emails, Peggy introduced me
to her friend Lynn Misch, who with her husband,
Pastor Steve Misch, has regularly participated
in mission outreach efforts to the people of
Candelaria. Lynn graciously supplied me with
myriad details about this tiny Texas border town
and its people. While my story and characters
are purely from my imagination, the
ongoing needs in Candelaria are very real.

Special thanks to my editor, Melissa Endlich, and
her staff for the opportunity to share this story
with Love Inspired readers. Also to the ladies
of Seekerville (seekerville.net) for sharing their
wisdom and experience through the publication
of my first Love Inspired romance story.

Chapter One

The end of the road—that's what it felt like for Ben Fisher.

Not literally, of course. Alpine, Texas, was some seventy or eighty miles from the Mexican border. Touristy chic in a Western, high-desert kind of way. Big Bend country, seasoned with the flavor of Mexico.

An interesting town, and a place Ben truly enjoyed visiting. He and his older brother, Aidan, had spent many summer vacations pretending to be cowboys and exploring their aunt and uncle's ranch outside town.

The only problem this time? A prolonged stay in Alpine, Texas, was *not* on Ben's current agenda.

Or it hadn't been until two weeks ago, when a memo from the Home Tech Revolution CEO changed the course of Ben's life.

He paused in the shade of a bright blue awning and gazed unseeing into a shop window along Holland Avenue. He'd already browsed through several gift shops, art galleries and specialty boutiques, none of which piqued his interest. Mucking stalls and hefting hay bales might be more therapeutic, but between Aunt Jane's concerned glances and Uncle Steve's penchant for handing out unwanted advice, Ben had needed to get away from the ranch for a while.

Except he'd slightly overdressed for a leisurely walk around downtown Alpine. When sweat threatened to soak through his maroon polo shirt, he decided to step in out of the September heat. As he pushed open the shop door, a blast of chilly air raised goose bumps on his arms. He dodged a string of jangling brass bells, but one managed to slap him in the forehead anyway.

"Ouch." He rubbed the spot as he nudged the door closed with his elbow.

"Sorry." A young woman appeared from the back of the shop. She wore a dark blue apron over jeans and a T-shirt, her straight auburn hair pulled into a ponytail. "The bells are a new addition. Guess I didn't consider my taller customers."

At barely six feet, Ben didn't consider himself particularly tall for a guy. He arched a brow. "You usually cater to munchkins?"

"This time of year, yes." The woman was almost Ben's height, even in her sneakers. She nodded toward a nearby counter, where a placard announced an upcoming after-school photography class for children. "I take it you aren't here to enroll your child?"

"Uh, no. I mean, I don't have any kids. I'm not even—" Ben clamped his teeth together and forced an apologetic grin. "Truth is, I just stepped inside to cool off."

"Oh." She sounded so disappointed that Ben almost wished he did have a kid to sign up for her class.

Almost. Marriage and family remained way down his list of priorities—and would until he got his career back on track.

Barely disguising a sigh, the attractive proprietor stepped across the room and reached up to straighten a poster-size framed photograph of a little girl climbing onto a school bus. A long, black braid swung down the child's back. The photo had captured the girl as she peered over her shoulder with a wistful, world-weary smile.

Only then did Ben take a serious look at his surroundings—another art gallery. More accurately, a photography studio. A few cityscapes and landscapes were displayed, along with portraits of children and teens, family groups and wedding parties. Typical professional photography fare.

But as he browsed the wall where the picture of the little girl hung, Ben felt as if he'd stepped into another world. These photos captured real people doing everyday things. Kids swatting at a piñata. An elderly woman knitting. Two boys playing catch. And most of the subjects appeared to be Hispanic.

He stepped closer. As a promotion manager—okay, *former* promotion manager—he knew more than a little about photography and composition. Whoever snapped these pictures had talent. He slid his gaze to the young woman. "You take these?"

She offered her hand. "Marley Sanders, at your service."

"Ben Fisher. Pleased to meet you." He noted her confident grip. If he still had his job back in Houston, he'd have wasted no time asking for her portfolio so he could present it to the ad team. "Even if I don't have a kid to sign up, is it okay to look around?"

"Be my guest." Marley looked at her watch. "For fifteen minutes, anyway. I'm closing at four so I can get to a meeting."

"Ah, a woman with an agenda. Okay, I'll hurry." Hands in his pockets, Ben moved along the wall, each photograph more impressive than the one before. "Are these for sale?"

"Sure!" An eager response if Ben had ever heard one. She cleared her throat. "I mean, yes, anything you see here is available for purchase. I also have a number of photos on display at various businesses around town, so if you don't see anything you like—"

"I see plenty I like." Ben studied a photo featuring a bright red portable building shaped like a barn. The double doors stood open, and inside a young Hispanic mother with a baby on her hip perused shelves lined with canned goods and other grocery items. He doubted this woman ever shopped at Home Tech Revolution. He glanced at Marley over his shoulder. "Interesting subject. Is this somewhere around here?"

"It's a little town called Candelaria, about ninety miles west." A faraway look darkened her dusky brown eyes even more. Anticipation? Concern? Ben couldn't tell. "Most of the photos in this group were taken there. It's a special place."

"Must be, if you've spent so much time photographing it."

"It's not just the town. The people are amazing—" The chirping of a cell phone interrupted her. She slid an iPhone from her back pocket. "Hi, Pastor. On my way right now."

Ben started toward the door. "Guess you need me to clear out."

"Sorry. I didn't realize how late it was. Watch out for the—"

Too late. As Ben pulled open the door, the brass bells bounced off and beaned him again.

"Oops." Behind him, Marley tittered. "I really need to shorten those things."

"Or up your liability insurance." Shooting her a wry smile, Ben stepped onto the sidewalk. "Nice meeting you, Marley Sanders. You do good work."

She wiggled her fingers in a tentative wave before locking the glass door behind him. Pointing at the dangling string of bells, she mouthed, *Gone tomorrow. Promise.*

He gave her a thumbs-up and decided a brief stay in Alpine might be exactly what his bruised ego needed.

Wow, nice guy. Except why couldn't he have been a nice *dad* enrolling his kid in Marley's photography class. She needed at least four more registrants just to break even. The absolute last thing she wanted to do was go to her father again for another infusion of capital. His subsidies were always secret, naturally, since Missouri State Representative Harold Sanderson had a reputation to protect.

Exactly why she'd moved a thousand miles away to Alpine, where no one knew her as anyone but Marley Sanders.

How many years had she worked to make it on her own, to prove to herself and her parents that she could live a responsible, productive, meaningful life? Her messed-up past was marred by lousy high school records and too many appearances in juvenile court. But the one mistake that finally brought her to her knees was a tragic auto accident that left Tina Maxwell, her one true friend, in a coma for six weeks.

With so much going against her, Marley had had no choice but to let Mom and Dad pay her way through college. She'd chosen Sul Ross State University in Alpine because of its remote West Texas location, then fell in love with the area and the people and decided to stay.

During her college years she became interested in photography. After she graduated, her father continued to send money while she got her studio up and running. But income remained sporadic, and more than once her father had not so subtly suggested she might want to switch to a more lucrative career.

That is, *if* he contacted her at all.

Time to stop dwelling on the past. She couldn't change it anyway, so the most she could hope for was to live purposefully in the present and try to make a difference.

And make her business profitable enough so she could stop depending on Daddy's money.

Maybe the nice Mr.—what did he say his name was? Fisher. Maybe Mr. Fisher would come back tomorrow and actually buy one of Marley's photographs. He sure seemed interested. Even looked as if he could afford her prices, judging from his designer-label polo shirt and neatly pressed khakis.

Oh, and the trendy haircut. Short but spiky, like one of those intentionally messy movie-star dos, and an interesting shade of light brown mixed with hints of sun-kissed blond. His hair color looked natural, but Marley knew plenty of women who'd pay their stylists big bucks to get such attractively subtle highlights.

Yep, the dapper Mr. Ben Fisher was definitely an out-of-towner, and since not many locals actually bought her stuff, all the more reason she needed to rely on income from her commercial photography and children's classes.

After flipping around the Closed sign in the front window, Marley turned off the lights, ditched her apron and headed out the back door. She jogged to the small parking lot at the end of the alley, then climbed into her ancient green Honda Civic and drove across town to the church.

By the time she sidled into the library and found an empty chair at the conference table, Pastor Chris's Spirit Outreach meeting appeared to be well under way.

"Glad you made it, Marley." Pastor Chris tapped a pen against his legal pad, which was propped on the edge of the table. "We're discussing ways to step up our outreach efforts."

Marley's friend Angela Coutu, seated across the table, spoke up. "Which isn't easy, considering the size of our congregation. We're doing all we can."

"We could do more," her husband, Ernie, said. "I'd like to see us affiliate with an organization like Big Bend Assistance Alliance. They're doing amazing work in the cities where they're active."

Marley tapped her nails on the tabletop. "Too bad they don't have a branch in Alpine."

"I hear they're looking into it," Pastor Chris stated. "But it'll be after the first of the year at the earliest, and we've still got two Candelaria trips to organize between now and Christmas. We need to think about fund-raising, getting supplies together and rounding up volunteers."

Straightening, Marley folded back the cover on her tablet computer. "We've got the next work trip covered for volunteers, right?" She had really wanted to go along but couldn't break away from the studio that week. At least she could look forward to the trip the week before Christmas, when several college students from a Texas Tech campus ministry would join them.

Discussion continued, and with the work trip details finalized, the committee talked more about their Christmas plans for Candelaria.

Running a hand across his crew cut, Pastor Chris checked his notes. "The Texas Tech group will be doing some fund-raising on campus between now and the end of November, and the director's counting on seven or eight students to sign up for the holiday mission trip."

"That'll be a big help." Marley typed the number 8 and a question mark next to "visiting mission team" in her planning list. "I think we should consider a major fund-raiser of our own, though. I want to give those kids and their families a really special Christmas."

Judy Jackson, a silver-haired retired teacher, flipped backward through her spiral notebook. "In the past, we've done things like car washes, pancake breakfasts, and church-wide garage sales. Those are all fine and dandy, but if we want continued support from the community, we need to come up with something original."

An hour later, the Spirit Outreach committee

had tossed out several ideas for possible fund-raisers, none of which the entire group could agree on. Some were too complicated, others too corny, and by the time Pastor Chris adjourned the meeting, Marley's frustration level had reached its peak. She'd grown so fond of the little town and its people, and all she wanted was to put an end to the haggling and do something tangible to help.

Pastor Chris walked Marley out to her car. "Hang in there. You know how committees work. We'll eventually get this figured out."

Marley answered with a smile and a shrug.

"How's your class sign-up coming?"

"Not good. I'd hoped for some return business from kids who took my summer classes, but I guess they lost interest."

"September's a busy time for parents. Maybe they'll get around to it once the kids settle into their school routines."

"Maybe." Marley didn't feel optimistic. She opened her car door and tossed her shoulder bag and tablet case across to the passenger seat. "Oh, well, if the class doesn't happen, I'll have more time to get ready for Candelaria." She gave a heartless laugh. "Not to mention I'll be saving money on utilities."

Pastor Chris leaned against the fender. A concerned frown creased his brow as he squinted against the afternoon sun. "You doing okay? Financially, I mean?"

Marley shrugged. "I'll make it." She climbed into her Civic, wincing as heat from the black vinyl upholstery penetrated her jeans. "Let me know when the next meeting is, Pastor. In the meantime, I'll work on the list of craft supplies the ladies asked for."

One hand braced on the door frame, Pastor Chris fixed Marley with a pointed stare. "Track your expenses, okay? We're taking up a special offering every Sunday this month, so we can reimburse you out of the donations."

"I will, I promise." Marley couldn't afford to do otherwise, but she looked forward to the day when she could give more than just her time and talent to the cause she cared so much about.

"Ouch!" Ben was beginning to wish he'd worn a crash helmet for his trip into Alpine.

True, he should have taken the last dip a little slower. Uncle Steve had warned him the ranch road didn't offer the best driving conditions for Ben's low-slung cherry-red Mustang convertible. Rubbing his head with one hand and gripping the steering wheel with the other, he eased off the accelerator. On this washboard of a road, speed was not his friend.

The western sky had darkened into breathtaking shades of purple, gold and magenta by the time Ben pulled up next to his uncle's stone-and-cedar ranch house. Stepping from the Mustang, he glimpsed Uncle Steve watching from a front-porch rocking chair.

"Thought I might have to send out a search party." His uncle moseyed down the porch steps. "Have a good day exploring the city?"

City? Houston was a city. Dallas was a city. Ben might even call Abilene a city. As for Alpine... Ben shrugged. "Looks pretty much the same. Except maybe even more artsy-craftsy than I remembered."

"The artist community does bring in tourists." Uncle Steve motioned Ben to one of the rockers. "Aunt Jane's fixing supper. Want an iced tea while we wait?"

Nothing sounded better. Even with the Mustang's windows shut tight and the A/C set to recirculate, Ben's mouth tasted as if he'd swallowed dirt all the way from town. While his uncle went inside to fetch a glass, Ben settled into a rocking chair and gazed toward the rugged mesas and distant mountains stretching across the horizon. He could already feel a difference in the air temperature as the sun slipped lower. One extreme to the other.

Just like Ben's life.

The screen door banged, and Uncle Steve

passed Ben a frosty tumbler of iced tea before returning to his chair. "Jane says fifteen more minutes. We weren't sure when you'd get back."

"You didn't have to wait. I'm used to fending for myself." Ben tossed back a big gulp of tea and let the coolness wash the dust from his throat. He liked Aunt Jane's special blend, with hints of mint and citrus and sweetened just right.

Uncle Steve looked askance at Ben's khakis. "Son, when are you gonna get yourself a regular ol' pair of blue jeans? You go around dressed like a city slicker and folks around here are liable to laugh you straight back to Houston."

"I have jeans." Ben's reply sounded whiny, even to his own ears. He rocked harder. "Just haven't unpacked them yet."

Glancing toward Ben's dust-coated Italian loafers, Uncle Steve snickered. "Might want to get yourself some boots, too."

The rocker stopped. With a barely suppressed grin, Ben slowly swiveled his head toward his uncle. "Yes, sir. Let me know when you're through criticizing my wardrobe."

A moment later, Aunt Jane pushed open the screen door. "Chow's on the table, boys. Y'all come on in and wash up." She patted Ben on the shoulder as he stepped through the door. "Don't pay that old coot any mind. It's nice to have a man around here who shows a little class."

"Thanks, Aunt Jane. And for the record, I think you're one classy lady." He tweaked one of her platinum curls before following her to the kitchen.

Unfortunately, Uncle Steve was right. Here at the ranch, Ben's casual-Friday slacks and Ferragamo loafers were the height of impracticality. He'd noticed the pretty photographer eyeing his attire as well—probably seeing dollar signs and hoping he'd snap up one of her photos.

If she only knew how fast his bank account was dwindling. Not that he was anywhere near destitute—he'd been careful to sock away hefty chunks of his salary into savings—but with no idea how soon he'd be employed again, he couldn't afford to be frivolous.

Ben took the chair at the opposite end of the table from his uncle and breathed in the zesty aromas of homemade enchiladas, Spanish rice and cheesy refried beans. "Wow, Aunt Jane, you could open your own restaurant."

She laughed as she refilled Ben's iced-tea glass. "Honey, I've got my hands full riding herd over your fool of an uncle."

"Pass me your plate, boy," Uncle Steve said, reaching across the table, "and I'll serve you up some grub."

Aunt Jane's enchiladas tasted as good as they smelled. She hadn't skimped on the jalapeños, either. Ben was no stranger to hot-as-you-can-handle Tex-Mex, but by the time he'd polished off a third helping, he could almost feel the smoke pouring from his ears. He huffed and puffed and fanned his mouth. "Anybody got a fire extinguisher?"

"Milk's the best thing." Laughing, Aunt Jane rose and took a glass from the cupboard.

As soon as Ben gulped the ice-cold milk, the pain subsided. He patted his full belly and leaned back. "I mean it, Aunt Jane. With you as chef, we could go into the restaurant business and make a mint."

Both his aunt and uncle chuckled and shook their heads, and Ben didn't have the guts to tell them he was half-serious. He desperately needed to come up with *some* kind of plan to jump-start his stalled career. Nothing in a million years could have prepared him for getting laid off from his dream job. Just proved how naive he was, assuming a thriving brick-and-mortar chain like Home Tech Revolution was immune to the growing trend toward internet shopping.

After helping with the dishes and putting away leftovers—barely enough for someone's meager lunch, after the damage Ben had done—Ben collapsed on the leather sofa in the great room and kicked off his loafers. While Uncle

Steve flipped satellite channels on the big-screen TV, Aunt Jane pulled out some kind of yarn thing to work on. The quick action of her fingers mesmerized Ben.

He raised on one elbow for a better look. "What are you making?"

"It's a baby blanket." Aunt Jane's eyes sparkled over her silver-rimmed reading glasses. "We have a ministry at church where several ladies knit afghans, prayer shawls and the like for people who have a special need or could just use something soft and comforting in their lives."

"That's nice." He wasn't really sure what a prayer shawl was, but then lately he hadn't had much practice with prayer. These days he wasn't on very good terms with God.

"This blanket's for a sweet young mom in Candelaria."

It was the second time today Ben had heard the name. He pictured the photo of the mother and child selecting food items in the little red barn. He sat up again and planted his feet on the floor. "You wouldn't by chance know the photographer in town with all the pictures of Candelaria."

"Marley?" Aunt Jane looked up with a smile. "She's a doll. And so dedicated to helping the families out there."

Uncle Steve turned down the TV volume. "Did you find Marley's gallery while you were in town?"

"Yeah, I happened upon it. She's really talented."

Aunt Jane and Uncle Steve exchanged glances, then nodded as if sharing some secret communication. Uncle Steve grinned at Ben. "Son, we just might have some ideas to put you to work while you're here."

Ben didn't know whether to be grateful or scared. Then the possibility of seeing Marley Sanders again took hold, and he felt the first twinges of anticipation he'd experienced in weeks.

Chapter Two

"Your total comes to sixty-three dollars and eighty-four cents."

Marley offered a tight-lipped smile as she fished her debit card from her wallet and ran it through the scanner. The cashier stuffed Marley's craft supplies into three plastic bags, then handed her the receipt. She tucked it next to her cell phone so she wouldn't forget to give it to Pastor Chris after church tomorrow.

Otherwise, especially after the notice she'd received from her studio landlord yesterday, she might be eating cold cereal three times a day for the foreseeable future. The landlord had decided to give the buildings on her block a face-lift, which meant a rent increase beginning in January.

With less than four months to raise her profits, where was her wealthy patron of the arts when she needed him? Apparently, Mr. Designer-Label Fisher had better uses for his money than returning to purchase one of the photos he'd admired yesterday. Since she'd even kept her promise to shorten the string of bells, Marley couldn't suppress a sad chuckle.

But why expect this guy to be any different from the usual tourists strolling through the arts district? They mostly just browsed anyway. Despite frequent assurances they'd stop in again after shopping around, few ever did.

In the shopping center parking lot, Marley tossed the bags in the trunk of her Civic, then settled behind the wheel and started the engine to get the A/C running. While the hot air blasting her face gradually cooled, she pulled out her phone to check messages and email. Surely there'd be at least one more registration for her photography class.

Nothing.

She tipped her head against the steering wheel and groaned. *Dear God, don't make me break down and call my dad.*

Maybe she'd drive by the church right now and see if Pastor Chris or his secretary happened to be in the office on a Saturday morning. She didn't look forward to scrounging through the meager leftovers in her fridge to find something for tonight's supper.

As she started to back out of her parking space, a car horn blared behind her. She slammed on the brakes. In the rearview mirror she glimpsed a flashy red convertible with the top down. A guy in smoky aviator sunglasses glowered at her from the driver's seat before gunning his engine and swinging into the empty space on her right.

Marley groaned. Must be another wealthy out-of-towner. She couldn't resist an annoyed glance as the driver opened his door. At least he took care not to bump her car. More likely, he was trying not to scratch his own.

Then he caught her eye through the window. Oh, no, the trendy-haircut guy? Marley's breath hitched.

He must have recognized her, too. Grinning, he whipped off his sunglasses and motioned her to roll down her window.

"Can't," she answered with a shrug, hoping he could hear her through the glass. "It's broken."

He nodded and stepped around to her door while she lowered the driver's-side window. "Marley, right? Remember me? Ben Fisher."

"Of course." Ben Fisher wasn't exactly a forgettable kind of guy. "Don't tell me you're here to shop? I pegged you for more of a Saks Fifth Avenue type. If we had one of those around here."

His grimace told her she'd touched a nerve.

"Since it looks like I could be around awhile, thought I'd stop in at the local department store to pick up a few T-shirts and maybe a pair of sneakers." A funny smile stole across his lips. "According to my uncle, I gotta quit dressing like a city slicker or risk getting laughed out of town."

Marley couldn't resist giving him the once-over. Another slim-fitting polo shirt in a mossy shade of green complemented his tan. The khakis were gone, but his citified jeans and the same polished loafers made him look more country-club than country.

"He's right, isn't he?"

Swinging her gaze back to his face, Marley winced as heat rose in her cheeks. "I'm sorry—who are we talking about?"

"My uncle."

"Oh, right." Maybe this was a conversation better continued at eye level. Marley stepped from the car and folded her arms. "So you're here visiting your uncle?"

"He has a ranch a little ways out of town. He says he knows you."

As long as she'd lived in Alpine, Marley had never quite gotten over the twinge of anxiety such a statement always evoked. She tried to mask the tension in her tone. "What's his name?"

"Steve Whitlow."

A wave of relief washed over her. "Yes, Steve and Jane—great people. We don't attend the same church, but they're regular supporters of our Candelaria outreach."

"So I've been told." Ben cocked a hip. "Like I said, I'll probably be around awhile, so Uncle Steve thought maybe I could help with whatever you're doing out there."

The way his voice dipped suggested he wasn't exactly thrilled about the idea. Marley lifted her chin. "I appreciate the offer, but if you're looking for something fun and exciting to do while you're in town, Candelaria isn't it."

Hands upraised, Ben took a step back, his expression hardening. "Believe me, fun is the *last* thing on my mind at the moment."

"I'm sorry. It just sounded like—"

"No, *I'm* sorry. Guess I'm a little touchy these days." He sighed and attempted a smile. "You were just leaving. Don't let me keep you."

"Yeah, and you have some shopping to do." Relaxing a little, Marley couldn't resist a smirk.

Ben tapped his aviators against his thigh as he studied her. "You have somewhere else to be right now?"

"Nowhere special." Why did she just say that? Did she want to blow any chance of catching someone in the church office this morning? "Why do you ask?"

Nodding toward the store entrance, Ben shrugged. "I was thinking I could use a little fashion advice."

"I don't know…"

"Please? You don't want me embarrassing my aunt and uncle, do you?" He nudged her out of the way of her car door and pushed it shut. "Come on, give me half an hour and I'll buy you lunch."

Marley narrowed her gaze. "Restaurant of my choice?"

"You name the place."

"City slicker, you've got yourself a deal."

Ben couldn't believe he'd just asked a girl to lunch.

Or that she'd accepted.

Not a date exactly, but as close as he'd come in a long, long time. His climb up the career ladder hadn't left much time for a social life. Maybe his meteoric crash into unemployment had an unexpected perk.

Or so he thought until he read the menu prices at the restaurant Marley selected. He smirked. "You have excellent taste, Miss Sanders."

Her pupils darkened as she studied the entrées, and he could swear she was actually salivating. "For obvious reasons, I don't come here often." She peered over the menu and wiggled her brows. "But you did say I could pick anywhere I wanted."

"I certainly did." Ben returned his attention to the menu. Maybe he'd settle for a salad. And water.

At least he'd gotten out of the department store without breaking the bank. Three colored T-shirts, two pairs of Wranglers, a package of tube socks and a pair of heavy-duty sneakers. Plus a nifty gray ball cap. Marley had reminded him that, even with the approach of fall, the high-desert sun could be brutal. And all his purchases amounted to less than what he typically paid for his favorite brand of dress slacks.

Or Marley's meal, apparently. She went all out, ordering an appetizer, salad, ten-ounce rib eye and baked sweet potato with all the trimmings.

Ben narrowed his gaze. "Skipped breakfast, huh?"

She shot Ben a sheepish glance as she passed her menu to the server. "I'll probably take half of it home."

"Now I'm subsidizing your grocery budget?"

Marley gave a playful sniff. "It's the least you can do, since you never came back to buy one of my photographs."

"I wish I could. It's just—"

The server cleared his throat. "Sir? Have you decided?"

"Chopped salad, balsamic vinaigrette on the side." Closing his menu, Ben motioned toward the miniature loaf of dark bread the server had brought with their waters. "And can we have a couple more of those?"

"Salad? That's all you're having?" Marley grimaced. "You must think I'm a glutton."

"Not at all." Ben sliced off a thick piece of bread and slathered it with butter. "I realize my city-slicker duds probably made you think I'm loaded."

Marley harrumphed as she buttered a slice for herself. "Not to mention your fancy red convertible."

"The truth is, I was laid off two weeks ago. If I don't find another job soon, it may come down to selling the Mustang so I can pay my rent—on a *much* smaller condo."

"I'm sorry. I had no idea." Marley shot an embarrassed glance around the restaurant. "If you can find our waiter—"

"Forget it. I'm not broke yet." Ben paused to savor a mouthful of warm bread oozing with melted butter, then wiggled his brows. "Anyway, I owe you for helping me pick out my swanky new wardrobe."

"Still, I'd have been just as happy with a burger and fries at the DQ." Marley stared guiltily at her bread slice before nibbling a tiny bite.

"Yes, but the ambience here is so much nicer." Not to mention the view across the table. Marley wore her hair down today, and Ben liked the way it framed her face. He imagined touching those silky auburn strands...

Suddenly the clinking of tableware and the conversations of other diners seemed amplified a hundred times. Ben blinked and buttered another piece of bread. No point in starting something he couldn't finish, seeing as how he didn't envision sticking around Alpine once he found another job. He was only here for some R and R. A rented beach house on Galveston Island would have been his first choice, but Uncle Steve and Aunt Jane had offered free room and board.

The server returned with Marley's appetizer, a platter of cheese quesadillas. She nudged it toward Ben. "Have all you want. You're buying, after all."

"Don't mind if I do." As Ben helped himself, he watched Marley scrape the *pico de gallo* off hers. "Not into hot and spicy?"

She slurped up the melted cheese dripping from her quesadilla, then shook her head. "Not even after ten years in Texas."

"Ten years? I took you for a native. Where are you from?"

At that exact moment, Marley stuffed the rest of her quesadilla into her mouth. Making exaggerated chewing motions, she waved her hand to signal she couldn't answer yet. Ben spooned her unwanted *pico de gallo* onto another quesadilla and polished it off while he waited. He didn't think she'd ever finish chewing and swallowing.

When she finally did, she must have forgotten his question. "Were you serious about getting involved with the Candelaria ministry?"

Ben sipped his water. "Sure. What exactly do you do?"

"All kinds of stuff. I was at the craft store to pick up supplies for the ladies. A while back, a fabric store donated several sewing machines, and the ladies create some lovely handcrafts. Then several state-park gift shops sell the items on consignment."

Marley went on to tell how college students from Austin had built the little red barn he'd seen in the photograph. "It's a reimbursement store stocked by volunteers, and one of the local women manages it. Everything is sold at cost, so they don't have to deal with the whole sales-tax issue."

Ben squinted in disbelief. "Wait—you're telling me there's nowhere else in Candelaria to buy necessities?"

"They have nothing. No stores, no gas stations, not even a real school anymore. The nearest town with shopping and schools is fifty miles away."

"Then why don't they—"

The server interrupted him to deliver their salads. Ben drizzled dressing over the lettuce and was about to pick up his knife and fork when he noticed Marley folding her hands.

"Do you mind if I offer grace?"

He should be used to this. Aunt Jane and Uncle Steve gave thanks before every meal, just as Ben's parents had always done. Mealtime prayer was a ritual he'd let slide sometime during college. Guess he'd grown too complacent relying on himself to give the Lord any credit. But then, God had let Ben down too many times in the past couple of years.

Awkwardly, he dropped his hands to his lap and waited while Marley whispered a simple but heartfelt prayer. Her ease with the words and the intimate tone of her voice suggested she felt totally comfortable conversing with the Lord.

She finished, and Ben retrieved his fork. He almost hated to break the reverent silence. "That was…nice."

Marley smiled as she took a bite of salad.

"Before the waiter came, you were about to ask me something."

It took him a moment to remember. "You said there's nothing in Candelaria. So why don't the people just move to a bigger town?"

"First of all, no one ever talks about who or how many, but it's likely some of these families crossed over illegally, so Border Patrol keeps a close eye on anyone coming or going. For another reason..." Marley pushed a tomato around her salad plate, her expression suggesting he could never understand. "Candelaria is home to these people. Whole families have grown up there or across the border in San Antonio del Bravo. They have pride in their history, a connectedness to their roots that—"

She broke off abruptly and squeezed her eyes shut.

"Marley?" Ben stretched his hand across the table to touch her wrist. His chest tightened when a tear slipped down her cheek.

With a self-conscious laugh, she dabbed her face with her napkin. "Guess you can tell I'm rather passionate about this subject."

Ben had the feeling her tears stemmed from something deeper than altruism, but he didn't know her well enough to pry. He was thankful the waiter returned at that moment to serve Marley's entrée.

"Do you need any steak sauce, ma'am?"

"No, thanks. I'm sure it's fine." Anticipation filled her eyes, now as big as her dinner plate. She sliced off a juicy bite of rib eye.

The tempting aroma of seared meat eclipsed any appetite Ben had for chopped salad. Fisting his knife and fork, he pinned Marley with his best imitation of a John Wayne stare. "Little missy, if you're plannin' on takin' home any leftovers, you better guard that slab of beef with your life."

Marley left the restaurant with a container packed with three quesadilla triangles, half her dinner salad, most of her baked sweet potato and *maybe* enough steak for a meager sandwich. Poor Ben. She'd finally taken pity on him and offered a few bites of her rib eye. He acted as if he'd died and gone to heaven.

Guilt still plagued her for picking one of the most expensive restaurants in Alpine. Ben should have told her sooner about losing his job.

On the other hand, she understood perfectly well about keeping certain parts of your life private. Thank goodness Ben hadn't pressed for details about her background. She'd much rather talk about Candelaria.

Except she'd almost blown it. Choking up like that? Good grief! At least Ben seemed to accept her explanation about the source of her tears. The truth was an ache with no cure.

They'd driven over separately, so Ben walked Marley over to her car. "Mind if we exchange cell-phone numbers?"

Her heart drummed out a few staccato beats. The cute city slicker wanted her number?

"I mean, in case you figure out anything I can do to help with your committee."

"Oh, right." She stifled a groan at her own foolishness. He was attractive and funny and easy to talk to, but struggling to make her business profitable, volunteering on the outreach committee and striving every day to keep her past in the past, she had no room for a man in her life. Besides, the moment he found another job, he'd be long gone.

They traded phones to enter their contact information, then Ben helped Marley into the car with all her leftovers. He grinned hopefully. "If you need any help finishing those off…"

Laughing, Marley opened the food container and passed Ben another quesadilla. "Here, have one for the road."

He ate it in two bites, then slammed a fist to his chest in mock gratitude. "Your kindness is exceeded only by your—"

"By *your* flair for the dramatic." Grinning, Marley slipped her key into the ignition and got the A/C running. "Goodbye, Ben. And thank you again for lunch."

"My pleasure." He tapped his phone as she pulled her door shut and mouthed, *Call me.*

She smiled and nodded, but a nagging inner voice told her getting involved with Ben Fisher, whether platonically on her Candelaria committee or otherwise, might be the biggest risk she'd ever take.

Chapter Three

"I've got Jacob and Bryan signed up, Mrs. Hunter. You can pay me at the first class. And thank you!" Marley did a quick victory dance as she ended the call. One of her church friends had caught her after worship yesterday and asked to get her daughter on the list. Now Marley needed only one more student for the class. Some people were notorious for waiting until the last minute, and with two weeks to go, things were looking up.

Mondays at the studio were usually quiet, which gave Marley time to work in the darkroom. She liked the ease and convenience of digital photography, but for her gallery pieces, nothing beat large-format film she processed and printed herself.

Today she needed to select and print several landscape shots commissioned by a Texas travel magazine. The sooner she turned those in, the sooner she could cover next month's rent on the studio. Artistic photography may be her first love, but magazine work, family portraits, senior class photos and weddings paid the bills—at least for now.

Her thoughts drifted to the notice from her landlord. The studio was in a prime location for downtown foot traffic. The upside of moving to another part of town was lower rent. The downside? The old saying, "Out of sight, out of mind," might well hold true.

As she stood at the counter filling out the class registration for Mrs. Hunter's boys, the front door creaked open, barely disturbing Marley's shortened string of brass bells. A familiar face peered through the crack. "Is it safe?"

She feigned a sneer to disguise her unexpected pleasure at Ben's arrival. "Oh, please. Don't be such a wimp."

He slid the rest of the way inside while keeping one eye on the bells. "A guy can't be too careful around these parts."

Marley slid the registration form into the drawer, then circled the counter. "If you came back for the rest of the steak, you're about—" she counted on her fingers "—thirty-nine hours too late."

Ben chortled. "The way you were chowing

down Saturday, I'm surprised those leftovers lasted that long."

"They were sure good, though." Marley offered a sincere smile. "I mean it—thank you."

"You're welcome." Thumbs hooked in the pockets of the Wranglers Marley had helped him find, Ben turned to study her photos of Candelaria. "This is my favorite." He nodded toward the shot of the little girl boarding the school bus. "There's something about her expression, like she wants to but doesn't."

"Would *you* want to ride an hour and a half to and from school every day?" Marley stood beside Ben and recalled the morning she'd snapped the photo of Isabella Cortez. It was two years ago, the first day of school. "These kids want an education so badly, and they're all such good students. It's been a long, hard fight to get a school reestablished in Candelaria so the kids won't have to be bused into Presidio every day."

"There ought to be a better way." Frowning, Ben moved to another photo. "Like this little store. Can't they get a big-box store to come in?"

Irritation bristled. "Have I mentioned Candelaria is considered a ghost town? There aren't enough families in the area to support a convenience store, much less a major supermarket."

"Guess I've lived in the big city too long. Can't even imagine living under such conditions."

"Not many people can." Returning to the counter, Marley angled the photography-class poster a little more toward the front entrance. "Was there a particular reason you stopped in?" She peeked over her shoulder and wedged a touch of humor back into her voice. "Besides checking up on my leftover steak?"

"Actually, yes. Over the weekend I learned my aunt and uncle are about to celebrate their fortieth wedding anniversary. I'd like to give them something special and wondered if you'd do their portrait."

"Wow, forty years. In today's world, they're practically an endangered species." Marley tried not to think about her own parents, who'd separated not long after her dad decided to go into politics twelve years ago. Between the threat of divorce and his delinquent daughter with her juvenile record, Dad and his election team had their hands full doing damage control.

Then Mom had relented and promised to stick it out—if only for appearances' sake. With Marley, however, Daddy found it easier to quietly relocate her and change her name so he could pretend she never existed.

Until she ran short of funds. And dear old Dad wouldn't think of being late with a check for fear his little girl would reappear at the most inopportune moment to utterly humiliate him.

He couldn't seem to appreciate how desperately Marley struggled *not* to go to her father for assistance. Nor did he get the whole concept of turning one's life around, maybe because he had such a hard time doing so himself.

"Marley?" Ben's gentle tone drew her thoughts to the present. "You looked a million miles away."

"Just planning in my head what kind of portrait your aunt and uncle would like. I'm thinking a location shoot right there at the ranch."

"I like it. I could see the two of them on the porch swing, with the mountains in the background, maybe around sunset—"

"Hey!" Laughing, Marley waved her hands. "*I'm* the photographer, last time I checked."

Ben rested an elbow on the counter. His lazy grin did something to Marley's insides. "Isn't the customer entitled to offer suggestions?"

"Only if he doesn't get in the way of my creative vision." Marley crossed to the other side of the counter and pulled out her appointment book. "When do you want to do this?"

"I'll need to check with Uncle Steve and Aunt Jane. They don't even know about the idea yet."

"Just let me know. For a full-size portrait on canvas, I have to send the proof to a photo lab, which takes time." Marley laid a catalog on the counter and began flipping pages. "You need to decide what size portrait you want, then whether you prefer traditional stretched canvas or mounted on foam board. Then you have framing options—"

Eyes glazing, Ben raised his hands. "Why do I have a feeling this is going to be a lot more expensive than I bargained for?"

It happened every time. People came in wanting a family portrait or looking for a wedding photographer, and when Marley started talking prices, they looked as if she'd hit them with a stun gun. Would she ever get the hang of easing the client into the monetary portion of their discussion?

Pasting on a patient smile, she closed the catalog and slid it onto the shelf beneath the counter. "Don't sweat it. We have lots of options, and I'm perfectly willing to try to work within your budget."

"That's good, since I don't have one. I'm unemployed, remember?"

"Hard to forget, Salad Man." Marley winked. "I have an idea." She opened a drawer and brought out a gray vellum envelope. Inside was a blank gift certificate, which she laid on the counter in front of Ben. "We don't have to talk prices now, but I'll write in 'one professional portrait sitting and print,' and you can present it to your aunt and uncle. We'll figure out the rest later."

Ben ran his index finger along the certificate's silver border, then looked up at Marley with a grin. "This is perfect. Thanks."

His gaze held hers so long that she almost forgot how to breathe. She straightened and reached for her calligraphy pen. "All righty, then, I'll fix this right up for you."

Forty years. Ben had a hard time wrapping his head around the number. How did two people stay together so long, and look so happy doing it? But then, if Mom hadn't died, she and Dad would have celebrated their thirty-sixth anniversary this year. Ben and his brother, Aidan, used to be mortified by their parents' public displays of affection. Keith and Emily Fisher had had the kind of marriage Ben had always secretly wanted for himself someday.

And then came Paula. Thoughts of Ben's brassy new stepmother made Ben shudder worse than fingernails on a chalkboard. But when Dad chose to remarry so quickly, he hadn't asked for anyone else's opinion, least of all his own sons'.

All these thoughts played through Ben's mind that evening when he presented Uncle Steve and Aunt Jane the gift certificate Marley had prepared. Their enthusiastic response reminded him all over again why Steve and Jane were his favorite aunt and uncle. First they hugged him until he begged for mercy, and then they hugged and kissed each other like a couple of newlyweds.

"Sweetest thing anyone's ever done for us." Aunt Jane wiped tears from her eyes. "We haven't had a nice portrait done since our twentieth."

"Not counting those church directory pictures every few years." Uncle Steve grimaced. "Regular cattle call, the way they rush you in and out." He stroked Aunt Jane's cheek with a tender touch, his voice softening. "And last time they airbrushed away all my sweetheart's character lines."

"Character lines, my foot." Giving her husband a playful punch on the arm, Aunt Jane winked at Ben. "Sounds to me like your uncle needs a new pair of bifocals."

"I think you're gorgeous, Aunt Jane." Ben fetched the coffeepot and refilled everyone's mugs. As they returned to their seats around the kitchen table, he asked, "So, can we set up a time with Marley soon?"

Ben's aunt put a hand to the silver curls brushing her neck. "All depends on when I can get a salon appointment. If we're going to be preserved for posterity, I want to look my best!"

"I should have my suit dry-cleaned, too," Uncle Steve said. "Only ever wear it to weddings and funerals."

"No suits allowed." Ben smirked as he stirred hazelnut-flavored creamer into his decaf. "Seriously, I want to remember you just like you are today."

"Aw, Ben." His aunt patted his arm. "You've always been like a son to us. Having you around more than makes up for not having kids of our own. I'm glad your mama was willing to share."

"Me, too." Ben glanced away. Even two years later, he couldn't keep the lump from climbing into his throat. "I miss her."

"I miss her, too," Uncle Steve said, glancing away. "My little sister was the best."

The kitchen grew quiet for a few moments, and Ben couldn't stop thinking that God must really have had it in for him. First his mom's death, then Dad's remarriage. And now, on top of everything else, the career Ben had fought so hard for had been ripped away.

As if sensing he needed to change the subject, Aunt Jane picked up the gift certificate, a bemused smile tilting her lips. "Still can't get over you doing this for us. Marley's really going to set up her camera stuff out here?"

"The ranch landscape will be the perfect backdrop." Ben fought to shove down the niggling resentment, a side of himself he was growing to dislike more every day. "If we can decide soon on a date, she may be able to get it done before her after-school classes start up. Plus, it sounds like she's really busy with this mission outreach stuff."

Uncle Steve sipped his coffee. "I heard they're planning a trip to Candelaria the week before Christmas. Got a call from Marley's pastor over the weekend asking if we'd let them use our RV."

"You should join Marley's committee," Aunt Jane suggested. "I'm sure they could use someone with your business sense."

Ben scratched his head. "What do I know about church committees? Anyway, I should be spending my time job hunting."

Aunt Jane rose and began putting plates in the dishwasher. "I thought you were taking some time to regroup before you jump back into the job market."

"I can't put it off indefinitely." Ben carried his and Uncle Steve's empty coffee mugs to the sink. "I'm still paying rent on my Houston condo, and then there's my expensive toy sitting in your driveway." He nodded out the window toward his Mustang.

"Maybe you should let the condo go," Uncle Steve said. "You can stay with us as long as you like. Haven't I always said I'd turn you into a rancher someday?"

Ben couldn't help but laugh at his uncle's persistence. "You know I'm not cut out for country living."

Aunt Jane elbowed him. "Give it a chance and you might be surprised."

From the kitchen window, Ben glimpsed some of Uncle Steve's white-faced Herefords grazing in a nearby pasture. As boys, Ben and Aidan had visited a few times when their uncle had been preparing to ship cattle off to market. Ben always got attached to a favorite cow and hated saying goodbye when it came time to load the trailer. For weeks afterward he wouldn't touch a hamburger or steak, fearing it was his cow.

He had a sudden image of Marley Sanders wolfing down her rib-eye dinner, and he laughed out loud.

Ben spent most of the following two days combing job-search sites for anything in his field. His aunt and uncle's satellite internet connection wasn't the fastest, but he didn't have much choice unless he wanted to drive all the way into Alpine and find a coffee shop with free Wi-Fi.

He had to admit, though, the backyard view

while sitting at Aunt Jane's kitchen table sure beat the gray walls of his former office cubicle overlooking I-635. Rolling hills and rugged mesas dotted with desert plants, cattle grazing on stubby tufts of grass, a couple of horses cavorting in the near pasture—the Whitlow spread was a landscape straight out of a western film.

Uncle Steve entered through the back door and tossed his dusty straw Stetson onto a chair. "Having any luck?"

"Not much." Ben closed his laptop, then leaned back and stretched.

"Maybe it's time for a change." Uncle Steve grabbed a tall plastic tumbler from the cupboard, then filled it with crushed ice and water from the fridge dispenser. He took a big gulp and sat down across from Ben. "I'm serious, son. This layoff might be God's way of telling you He's got other ideas for your life."

"Then He should have told me before I invested all those years getting an MBA." Ben couldn't keep the sarcasm out of his tone.

"I'm not saying He doesn't intend for you to use the education and experience you already have. God doesn't waste anything." Uncle Steve's mouth twisted in a thoughtful frown. "But there could be other ways to use your skills besides sitting behind a desk in a high-rise office building."

Groaning, Ben ground his knuckles into his eye sockets. "I know you're trying to help, and I don't mean to sound ungrateful. But if you're trying to convince me to stay here and look for work in Alpine, it's not happening."

"Now hold on, Ben, and hear me out. I know you love it here. I know because you're like a different person, a happier person, every time you stay for a while. And like Jane and I have said time and again, you're like a son to us. So it'd mean the world to me if you'd consider— if you'd just *think* about—partnering with me here on the ranch."

Uncle Steve's words touched a deep place in Ben's heart, and it was true, he did love the ranch. Loved every minute he spent here. Blowing out a sharp breath, he scraped a hand down his face. "I can't even tell you what an offer like that means to me, Uncle Steve. But I just don't see it happening. You can put me in boots and jeans. You can trade in my Mustang for a bucking bronco. And I'll still be a confirmed city boy. It's who I am now. It's the only life I know."

Ben yanked the plug from the wall, grabbed up his laptop and trudged down the hall to the guest room.

Good jobs weren't about the view. Who had

time to notice the view, anyway, working fifty or sixty hours a week?

Ben flopped on the bed and stared at the ceiling. It was his father who'd suggested Ben spend a few weeks with Uncle Steve. He'd also made Ben promise he wouldn't even think about looking for work right away. "You're flush with savings," Dad had said. "Don't rush into anything. Use this time to get to know yourself again."

This from the man who obviously didn't know himself at all, who had remarried only nine months after Mom died.

And Uncle Steve certainly didn't know Ben if he honestly thought Ben was cut out for ranch management.

Someone tapped on his door.

"It's open."

Aunt Jane peeked in. "Just got back from town. I stopped in to see Marley and set up an appointment. She's coming out Sunday afternoon."

"Great." Ben sat up and shifted his legs off the side of the bed. He cast his aunt a sincere smile. "Your hair looks nice."

"Thanks for noticing." Aunt Jane patted her curls, a good two inches shorter than when she left that morning. "I'll be amazed if Steve even realizes I've been gone all day."

"He realized, all right, about the time he figured out we had to make our own lunch."

"Oh, that big ol' baby." Shaking her head, Aunt Jane stepped toward the hallway. "I'll start supper soon. Hope you like eggplant parmesan."

"Love it. Need any help?"

"Not right now. But you might give Marley a call. She mentioned the Spirit Outreach committee is having a workday on Saturday. Bet they could use an extra hand." With a wink, Aunt Jane sidled out the door and pulled it closed.

Thinking of Marley lightened Ben's mood. She'd certainly been a bright spot in his life lately. Since stopping in at her studio on Monday, he hadn't come up with a plausible excuse for another trip into town to see her. He found her name and number in his cell-phone contacts and tapped the call icon. "Hey, Marley. It's Ben."

"Hi." Her voice sounded breathy with surprise. "I saw your aunt earlier. We're all set for Sunday."

"She just told me. If there's anything you need me to do before then—"

"Maybe scout around for some fun places to shoot. I'd like to try several backdrops and lighting situations so they can pick what they like best."

"Will do." Ben toed the carpet. "Aunt Jane

mentioned you're having some kind of work-day this weekend. Need any help?"

"That would be great. A small team is going down to Candelaria next week to do painting and repairs on some of the homes, so we need to get supplies organized. If you're available, I'll put you to work."

Available didn't begin to describe Ben's current state. "I've got nothing better to do—" He cringed. "Wait, that didn't come out right."

Marley laughed. "Don't apologize. Just show up at 9 a.m." She gave him directions to Spirit Fellowship Church.

Ben snatched up a notepad from the night-stand and hurriedly copied down Marley's directions. "I assume jeans and T-shirt is acceptable attire?"

"If you show up in your designer polo and no-iron khakis, I will personally escort you off the premises," she teased.

"I'd like to see you try." In no hurry to end the call, Ben shifted some pillows and settled against the headboard. "You won't banish me if I arrive in my Mustang, I hope?"

Her tone became soft and flirty. "Not if you promise to take me for a spin after we're done."

"You're on."

They chatted a few more minutes about Saturday before Marley said a timer was going off in her darkroom and she needed to get back to work. Ben laid the phone on the nightstand and stretched out, hands folded behind his head. He should not be looking so forward to spending time with a girl who'd likely be out of his life in less than a month.

Unless you stay in Alpine.

His uncle's offer, impractical though it was, had somehow burrowed its way into Ben's brain. He'd have to be crazy to even consider it.

But then…getting laid off unexpectedly was enough to make any sane man go a little crazy.

Had she actually just *flirted* with Ben Fisher?

Marley checked the color balance on the landscape photo she'd just printed. Thanks to an advance from her dad a couple of years ago, she'd invested in a state-of-the-art film processor and could do her own developing. The creative control, not to mention the convenience, counterbalanced the discomfort of knowing her father had subsidized her photography business.

Too bad she didn't have the same control over her emotions. Hinting for a ride in Ben's cute red Mustang? What did she really expect to come of…whatever this was? Ben wasn't likely to stick around Alpine once he got his career back on course—which he wouldn't waste any time doing, if she read his signals correctly.

There was a restlessness about him that no amount of casual banter could hide.

But there was something more. Beneath his polished persona, Marley sensed a man of depth, commitment and concern. She'd seen it in his eyes as he'd studied the photo of Isabella climbing onto the school bus, and later as Marley had described the Candelarians' struggles. Ben truly cared.

Finishing up in the darkroom, she hung her apron on a hook and turned out the lights. Time to go home to her apartment and scrounge up something for supper. She smiled to herself, recalling the steak dinner she'd wheedled out of Ben. No steak tonight. Maybe some canned tuna, a boiled egg and a salad.

As she walked down the alley toward her car, her cell phone rang. A tremor of anticipation shot through her, and she wanted to kick herself for hoping it might be Ben. She took her time fishing the phone from her purse. If it *was* Ben, she certainly didn't want to sound overanxious.

The caller ID didn't give a name, but she recognized the St. Louis area code, and all traces of excitement fled. She answered with a tentative "Hello?"

"Marsha?"

"Mom." Calling on another of Dad's burner phones, obviously. Marley reached her car, glad as always to find it shaded by a building this time of day. She sank sideways into the driver's seat with the door open and her feet on the pavement.

"How are you, honey?"

"I'm fine. Why'd you call? Is something wrong?"

Silence, then… "Does there have to be something wrong? Can't I simply call to hear my daughter's voice? Please, Marsha—"

"It's Marley, remember? The daughter you *don't* have." She should be over this resentment by now. Hadn't she willingly agreed to the name change? Once upon a time, it had actually felt good to be free of all the baggage, to reinvent herself and start over as Marley Sanders.

Her mother whimpered softly into the phone.

"Please, Mom, don't cry. I'm sorry." Marley leaned forward to catch the light breeze. "Tell me what's going on there. Did Dad decide if he's going to run for another term?"

"Of course he will." Mom gave a disdainful sniff. "He's giving a talk to the Kiwanis Club this evening. I'm sure it'll turn into a political rally before he's done."

Here we go again. Marley's mother might put up a convincing front for their constituents, but she never hid her bitterness from Marley. Or Dad, either, most likely. "Are you going with him?"

"I'm pleading a headache." She sniffed. "Can we not talk about your father? I want to hear about you. How's your little studio doing?"

"Business is plodding along." She wouldn't mention the rent issue. Mom would only worry, and probably pester Dad about sending money. Marley didn't need another of his lectures about her incompetence as a business owner. Instead, she said, "My next kids' class starts a week from Monday."

"That's nice. And this…mission thing you're involved with? Are you going back to that dreary little town anytime soon?"

"Not until mid-December, but there's still plenty to do to get ready." Marley could tell her mother wasn't really interested. These phone calls usually only came when Mom's unremitting loneliness surfaced. She couldn't talk to her husband, and Marley's three older siblings learned long ago to separate themselves from their parents' drama. The Sandersons had also cut ties with the church they used to belong to, which was especially sad, because Zion Community Church had been one of the few positive influences in their lives. Now, even a thousand miles away, Marley had become her mother's primary support system.

More sniffling, then a choked sob. "Marsha, baby, I miss you so much! I wish you could come home."

"You know why I can't." Marley slid her legs beneath the steering wheel and leaned against the headrest. "Mom, I really have to go. I—I've got somewhere I need to be." *Home. Eating my tuna and salad. Alone.*

"Okay. But keep this number. I'll have this phone for a while, so call me sometime."

"Right. Sure." Marley squeezed her eyes shut, knowing she would never make the call. "I love you, Mom."

Chapter Four

Choosing a parking space outside Spirit Fellowship Church, Ben huffed a sigh of relief to see only a couple of other vehicles in the lot, one of them Marley's Honda. Unsure what to expect for a mission's committee workday, he'd arrived early, hoping Marley could ease him into this whole outreach thing. He didn't want to humiliate himself by doing or saying something stupid in front of her pastor and the other committee members.

As he stepped from the Mustang, a blue pickup pulled in a couple of spaces down on his left. A dark-haired guy in his late thirties wearing a beat-up Stetson climbed from the driver's side and strode around to the tailgate.

"'Mornin'," the man called with an appraising grin. "Nice wheels. Looking for someone?"

"I'm a friend of Marley's. She asked me to

come help with whatever they're doing today."
Holding his new gray ball cap behind him, Ben
nonchalantly scraped it along the side of his car
where road dust had collected. He wished he'd
thought to scuff up his sneakers, too, so they
didn't scream "new" so loudly.

"Always use an extra hand." The man lowered the tailgate and tugged a box to the edge,
then dusted off his palms. He extended his right
arm. "I'm Ernie Coutu."

"Ben Fisher." Ben accepted Ernie's firm grip.
He glanced toward the pickup bed, crammed
with cardboard crates and paint buckets. "Need
help unloading?"

"That'd be great. These are Candelaria donations from a few businesses in town." Ernie
wrestled the nearest box into his muscled arms.
"We're storing everything in an empty Sunday-
school room. Grab whatever you can carry and
follow me."

Ben slapped on his ball cap and leaned into
the truck bed. He set his sights on a couple of
five-gallon paint buckets. Good grief, they had
to weigh nearly fifty pounds each! He managed
to get them out of the pickup, but after taking
only a few staggering steps, he let the cans hit
the pavement with a thud. Flexing his aching
fingers, he gasped several breaths.

"Ben, are you crazy?" Marley jogged toward

him. She towed a heavy-duty yellow wagon. "Set the paint in here."

So much for avoiding looking stupid. He massaged a cramping bicep. "Didn't realize they'd be so heavy."

Marley smirked. "I'm guessing it's been a while since you bought paint."

"You'd be right." Lifting the buckets one at a time, Ben hoisted them into the wagon. "Looks like room for one more. I'll toss one down to you from the pickup."

"Yeah, you do that." Grinning, Marley pulled the wagon over to the tailgate.

Ben glanced over his shoulder as he hauled himself into the pickup bed. Why did Marley Sanders have to look so gorgeous in denim capris and a pink-and-white-striped cotton top? He should not even be here, much less succumbing to an attraction that held no future for either of them. Giving himself a mental shake, he hefted another paint bucket and worked his way to the tailgate.

Before he could lower himself to the ground to move the bucket into the wagon, Ernie returned and grabbed the handle. "Careful, there. Wouldn't want you to hurt yourself."

"Thanks." Ben stifled a twinge of envy as Ernie effortlessly shifted the paint can into the wagon. *Note to self: find new gym.*

Or he could get back in shape lifting hay bales for Uncle Steve. His uncle certainly hadn't been shy about hinting he'd like to get Ben more involved in ranch work. Sure, it had been fun for Ben and his brother when they'd visited as kids. But moving to Alpine permanently? Working at the ranch full-time? Ben just didn't see that happening.

Hands on hips, Marley cocked her head. "You gonna stay up there all day?"

"Sorry, I zoned out for a sec." Ben eased to the ground but kept one eye on Ernie as the man effortlessly hauled the wagon toward the church building. "Still not real sure I should be doing this."

Mouth puckered, Marley glanced away. "I understand, really. If this isn't your thing—"

"I won't lie to you. It's been a long time since I've had anything to do with church." He should cut and run right now, while she offered him an easy out. But the disappointment in her eyes slashed through his belly, and the next words out of his mouth seemed as if they came from a complete stranger. "Hey, I may be slightly out of my element, but I'm teachable. Besides, it's for a good cause. How can I say no?"

Marley's expression relaxed, but a hint of worry still pulled at the corners of her eyes.

"Are you sure your aunt and uncle didn't guilt you into volunteering?"

"Let's call it applying a little positive pressure. No guilt involved." Hoping to convince her, Ben grabbed one of the smaller boxes out of the pickup bed. "Let's get this stuff unloaded. Lead the way to your storage room."

Two more trips, plus Ernie's help with the wagon, and all the supplies had been moved inside. Marley opened a cooler and passed around cold cans of soda, which they sipped while sitting on paint buckets in the small classroom. Ben couldn't resist glancing in Marley's direction to admire her long, tanned legs and the way the end of her ponytail feathered across her shoulders.

She caught him looking at her and smiled. "Sure glad you're here. I expected we might have a low turnout today, but I never dreamed it'd be just the three of us."

"Glad I could help." Ben's chest warmed, and he sat a little straighter. "After all the time I've spent behind a desk, it actually feels good to do something physical."

Ernie cleared his throat, reminding Ben he and Marley weren't alone. "What's next, Marley?" Ernie asked. "We need to inventory this stuff?"

Marley popped up from her paint bucket. "I'll get my list."

As Marley darted from the room, Ernie gave a low chuckle. "Thought you two had forgotten about me for a minute."

With a self-conscious laugh, Ben stood and pawed through the nearest box to see what it held. Paintbrushes, masking tape, stir sticks...

Ernie ambled over, and his voice dropped to a whisper. "Don't mess with Marley. You get my drift?"

Ben straightened. "Hey, if you two have something going—"

"Nothing like that. But hurt her, and you'll answer to the entire congregation of Spirit Fellowship." The smile never left Ernie's face as he spoke, but his humorless tone left no doubt he meant every word.

Ben lifted both hands in a defensive posture. "I'm only in town for a few weeks. You've got nothing to worry about."

"Let's hope not." Ernie glanced toward the door as footsteps sounded in the corridor.

Marley appeared, tablet computer in hand. Her confused gaze darted between the two men. "Did I miss something?"

"Just guy talk." Sliding a glance toward Ben, Ernie bent over a crate. "Got that list?"

While Ernie and Marley checked off the supplies, Ben stepped to one side and pretended to study a paint-bucket label. Ernie's warning shouldn't bother him as much as it did, especially since he had no intention of letting anything develop between him and Marley. Yeah, he found her attractive—and not just because of her unpretentious good looks. There was something special about Marley, something that made Ben think she was exactly the kind of girl he could go for.

If he weren't unemployed with no prospects on the horizon.

Which meant it wasn't fair to either of them to risk letting a casual friendship turn into something more. He should make some excuse and get out of here. Right now.

Then Marley's softly spoken plea froze him in his tracks. "Ben, I could really use your help."

Marley held her breath as she waited for Ben to reply. Her instincts told her he was ready to bolt, and she felt pretty sure it had something to do with whatever he and Ernie had talked about while she was out of the room.

Leave it to Ernie to act like her big brother with Ben. Like so many of her friends at Spirit Fellowship, Ernie and his wife, Angela, kept a close watch on Marley and made sure no one took advantage of her. Especially when it came to dating.

As if they had anything to worry about. Keeping her past private made Marley supercautious.

On the other hand, Marley didn't mind having Ben around while it lasted. She tried again. "How about it, Ben?"

He turned slowly, a resigned look flattening his expression. He reached for his soda can and drained the last few drops, then tossed it into a nearby garbage bin. "Whatcha need?"

"If you'll sort through the crates with us, we can finish a lot faster."

"Where shall I start?"

"Just pick a box. As we check things off, you can stack it on the other side of the room."

Ernie kept up a friendly chatter as they worked, but Marley couldn't help noticing Ben's silence. Was he *that* sorry the Whitlows had talked him into helping with the outreach team? She certainly didn't need a reluctant volunteer.

Nearing the end of her checklist, she stretched her tired back muscles. "That's pretty much everything. Ben, if you need to get out of here, Ernie and I can wrap this up."

Ben closed the flaps on the cardboard box he'd just set aside. "If you're sure…"

"No prob. We're almost done." Marley offered

an agreeable smile to cover the disappointment churning through her.

"Okay, then." Pulling a key ring from his pocket, Ben edged toward the door. "Guess I'll see you tomorrow."

Marley cast him a blank look. "Tomorrow?"

"The anniversary portrait. At my aunt and uncle's place."

With an embarrassed chuckle, Marley slapped her forehead. "Too much on my mind lately. I think I told Jane I'd be there around two o'clock."

"They're looking forward to it." Ben straightened his baseball cap. "Okay, then," he repeated. "See you tomorrow."

"See you." Marley's lungs deflated as Ben disappeared down the corridor.

Turning back to Ernie, she gave her checklist a final glance. "Looks like we're all set. Thanks for coming over this morning. Everyone else must be busy with family stuff."

Ernie brushed at some dust on his pant leg. "Nice that Ben could lend a hand."

Marley couldn't miss the unspoken question in his tone. "Don't get any ideas. He's just a new friend."

"Who'd like to be more, unless my radar's way out of whack."

With an exasperated sigh, Marley dug her

fists into her hips. "Ben's between jobs. He isn't interested in anything except filling time until someone hires him again."

"Coulda fooled me. I saw the way he looks at you."

Marley shut off the lights and stepped into the corridor. "You're imagining things. And by the way, what did you say to him while I was out of the room earlier?"

"I have no idea what you're talking about." Ernie pulled the classroom door shut behind them and made sure it was locked. "We should leave a note for Pastor Chris. He'll be glad to know we have most of the supplies accounted for."

"No hurry. He and Natalie went to visit her parents this weekend. Won't be back until Tuesday." Halting in front of the exit doors, Marley confronted Ernie. "And you're changing the subject."

Ernie shot her a butter-couldn't-melt-in-his-mouth grin. "Forgot there'll be a substitute pastor preaching tomorrow. Always nice to have Reverend Hinkhouse back in the pulpit."

"Er-r-r-nie." Marley's eyes became slits.

His shoulders slumped. "I told your city-slicker boyfriend he'd better not hurt you, or he'd answer to me and the entire congregation."

Chagrin knifed through Marley's abdomen. "Oh, Ernie, you didn't!"

Ernie's shoulders drooped. "You're like family, Marley, and the plain truth is I don't trust this guy. He's a rich out-of-towner with time on his hands, and that's the worst kind."

"You sound awfully judgmental for a Christian. Give Ben a break." Marley pushed through the doors and marched toward her Civic. She could only wonder how Ernie and the rest of the congregation would react if they ever got wind of her troubled past.

"Marley, wait up." Ernie jogged past her and skidded to a stop next to her car door. Frowning, he pawed the back of his neck. "I can see you like the guy. And you're right, it's not my place to pass judgment, especially since I just met him. But you hardly know him, either. Don't you think you should be a little bit careful?"

"Take my word for it, you have nothing to be worried about." Marley shook her head as she dug through her purse for her car keys. "Anyway, Ben is Steve and Jane Whitlow's nephew. I'm sure they'll vouch for his good character."

Ernie flinched. "The Whitlows? Why didn't you say so?"

"Why should I have to?" Marley reached past Ernie for the door handle. "Admit it, you had

Ben pigeonholed the minute you laid eyes on his Mustang. You never even gave him a chance."

"Okay, I didn't give him a fair shake. I apologize." Both hands lifted, Ernie backed away. "But do you really think he's gonna be much help with our outreach committee? I got a really strong vibe that he hasn't spent much time in church lately."

Marley pulled open the car door and tossed her things inside before pivoting to face Ernie. "Again, you are prejudging. And even if you're right about Ben, people can change. People can learn from their mistakes, repent and become better human beings. Isn't that why Jesus died for us?"

Ernie's lips quirked in a curious grin. "Maybe they should have asked *you* to fill in for Chris tomorrow, *Pastor* Sanders." Heaving a resigned sigh, he lowered his head. "And I totally get your point. Sorry for jumping to conclusions about Ben."

"I'm sorry, too." Marley grimaced. "Stepping off my soapbox now."

Turning toward his pickup, Ernie paused and snapped his fingers. "Almost forgot. Angela told me to invite you over for burgers tonight."

Relieved the tension had eased between them, Marley smiled her thanks. "Sounds great. I'll call Angela later and ask what I can bring."

They said their goodbyes, and Marley climbed into the Civic. With the air-conditioning cranked up, she drove toward her apartment, intending to freshen up and then open the studio. Weekends usually brought more shoppers to the arts district, and with the rent increase looming, she couldn't afford to miss out on any potential customers.

By the time she pulled into the parking space outside her apartment, she'd replayed her conversation with Ernie several times. *People can learn from their mistakes, repent and become better human beings.* Good grief, could she sound any more preachy? Not that she didn't believe every word she'd spoken, but it had less to do with Ben than with herself. She *had* repented after her juvenile delinquent past and become a better person, hadn't she? Candelaria was her atonement, her way of doing something good for others to make up for all the stupid, hurtful, downright dangerous things she'd done as a teen.

Yes, better to concentrate on the Candelaria outreach than to dwell on the past—worse, to entertain unrequited feelings for Ben Fisher.

Except now he'd volunteered to help with the outreach committee. He could still back out, though, and maybe he would. If he didn't, how would she ever stay focused?

* * *

As Ben parked the Mustang outside the garage, his uncle came around from the other side of the barn. Seeing Ben, he jogged over to the car. The crevices around his eyes were definitely from worry, not from squinting into the sun.

Ben unfolded himself from the low seat and slammed the car door. "What's up?"

"Ruby's down with colic. The vet's on his way, but Jane's gone shopping and I need help getting Ruby up and walking."

Ruby, Uncle Steve's favorite mare, had been around for almost as long as Ben could remember. He and Aidan had learned to ride on the gentle, patient roan, and now Ben was as worried as Uncle Steve.

When they reached Ruby's pasture, Uncle Steve grabbed a halter and lead rope off the gate and motioned Ben to follow him. A few feet inside the gate, the horse rolled and writhed, clearly in pain. Avoiding Ruby's lashing hooves, Steve tried to steady the horse's head long enough for Ben to fasten the halter. With Ben tugging on the lead rope and Steve muscling against Ruby's haunches, they urged her to her feet and got her walking around the pasture.

The vet arrived within minutes, and after examining the mare, he surmised Ruby hadn't been drinking enough water while she grazed. Uncle Steve led Ruby into her barn stall, where the vet began treatment. A stomach tube through the horse's nose was a little more than Ben could handle, though, so he observed from a distance.

Toting five-gallon paint cans and wrangling a colicky horse, all before lunch? Ben's muscles felt like jelly. Spying a tack trunk against the wall, he collapsed with a groan. This was a whole different kind of tired than sitting behind a desk forty or fifty hours a week.

He hadn't been sitting there long when the telephone rang inside the tack room. Since Uncle Steve was busy helping the vet with Ruby, Ben got up to answer the call.

It was Ernie Coutu. "Hi, Ben. We met this morning, remember?"

"Yeah, I remember." How could he forget?

"First off, I wanted to apologize if I came on too strong." Ernie released a self-conscious chuckle. "Marley reamed me out for it."

"I get it. You're just looking out for her."

"Right. So anyway, my wife, Angela, and I are throwing burgers on the grill tonight. Marley's coming, plus another couple from the outreach committee. I thought you might like to join us so we can all get better acquainted."

Ben glanced toward Ruby's stall, relieved to see the horse looking less stressed. Unlike him at the moment. "Sure, why not? Just tell me where and when."

Ernie suggested he arrive around five thirty. "Give me your cell number and I'll text you directions."

While the vet finished Ruby's treatment, Ben had another hour or so to stew about Ernie's unexpected invitation. He heard Aunt Jane's car drive up and went out to help her carry grocery bags into the kitchen.

When he told her he'd be having burgers at the Coutus', she beamed. "Glad I stopped at the bakery for *kolaches*. You can take some with you to share for dessert." She made a face. "But I strongly suggest you shower first."

Chuckling, he went to clean up. After lunch with his uncle and aunt, he stretched out on his bed for a short nap that lasted nearly three hours. Aunt Jane woke him with just enough time to drive into Alpine.

He parked in front of the Coutus' brick ranch-style house, and moments later Marley pulled up behind him. They stepped from their cars at the same time, and Marley nudged her door shut with one hip while juggling her purse, a bag of chips and what looked like a container of store-bought guacamole.

Answering the question in her eyes, he

grinned and said, "Blame Ernie. He isn't through analyzing my moral character."

He shifted the plate of *kolaches* to his other hand and relieved her of the dip she was struggling with. "Let me help."

"Thanks." She took a step back, then nodded approvingly. "Glad to see you didn't overdress for the occasion."

"I'm a quick study. Figured folks around these parts wear jeans and sneakers pretty much everywhere." Although Marley looked classy in black jeans, a paisley-print peasant top and strappy sandals.

Marley didn't bother ringing the doorbell but showed Ben straight through to the kitchen, where they left their meal contributions on the counter. The aroma of a charcoal fire drifted through the back screen door. They stepped out to the patio, and Marley introduced Ben to Ernie's wife, Angela.

The petite redhead rose and offered her hand. "Welcome. It's nice to finally meet you."

Another couple, Pete and Bonnie Oldam, arrived a few minutes later, and their two kids ran off to play on the swings with the Coutus' little girl. Angela brought more soft drinks from the cooler and the three couples sat around a glass-top patio table.

As the newcomer in the group, Ben got peppered with the usual questions about where he grew up, which college he went to and what he did for a living. Before it started feeling too much like an inquisition, he asked to hear more about the outreach ministry.

Instantly, the energy level around the table ramped up several notches. With everyone talking over each other, Ben could sit back and relax a little. At one point he realized he'd become riveted by Marley's animated use of her hands as she described the team's summer mission trip to Candelaria. She caught him looking at her, and with an embarrassed grin she dropped her hands into her lap.

"But that brings up another point," Ernie said. "If we're going to accomplish everything we want to by Christmas, we seriously need to decide on a fund-raiser."

Pete Oldam turned to Ben. "I bet with your background in advertising, you could be a big help with fund-raising ideas."

"Oh, no," Ben said. "Corporate promotions are a whole different animal from charity events."

"Besides," Marley said, "Ben's just visiting Alpine while he's between jobs. I'm sure he won't be around long enough to get involved with a fund-raiser."

Ben's sensitivity meter redlined again. He

thought he detected a tinge of resentment in Marley's tone. What he couldn't figure out was why. Hadn't he been completely up-front about his job-hunting intentions?

Angela tapped Ernie on the arm. "Sweetie, isn't the grill about ready? We should get the burgers started."

While Pete helped Ernie at the grill and Bonnie went inside with Angela to get the rest of the food, Ben drew Marley aside. "Am I making you uncomfortable by being here?"

"What? No, of course not." Marley forced a laugh, then shrugged. "I have a million other things on my mind, that's all."

"Anything I can help with?"

She counted off on her fingers. "You've already bought me an expensive lunch, carried paint buckets for the mission team and propped up my business with a portrait sitting for your aunt and uncle. Oh, and carried my guacamole. For a guy just in town for some R and R, I'd say you've gone well beyond the call of duty."

The breeze picked up suddenly, sending smoke in their direction. Coughing and fanning their faces, they stepped apart. Marley excused herself to help the ladies with the food, and Ben tried to look as if he knew something about grilling burgers. He'd certainly burned his share on his patio hibachi back in Houston.

Hanging out with the guys, though, with the kids romping on the lawn and the tempting aroma of sizzling beef in the air, made him miss similar times with his dad, brother and nephews. Would he ever get to experience the simple pleasures of family life for himself? Certainly not as long as everything revolved around his career.

But he had to make a living, didn't he? Raising a family these days wasn't cheap. Someday, when he'd saved enough, then maybe he'd be ready to settle down.

Chapter Five

After worship on Sunday, Marley hurried home to change into jeans and sneakers. She whipped up a berry smoothie for lunch and sipped it from an acrylic travel tumbler as she drove over to her studio. Letting herself in the back door, she made a quick stop in the darkroom to admire the wedding proofs she'd developed yesterday afternoon before going over to the Coutus'. Somehow she always needed to convince herself her pictures were as good as she first thought.

"Oh, yeah." Marley nodded as she studied the play of light and shadow in a black-and-white shot of the bride beneath a latticework arbor, a dreamy look in her eyes as if her sweetheart was just out of camera range. And he was, wisecracking until neither Marley nor the bride could keep from laughing out loud!

Yes, this shot was a keeper, definitely wall-worthy. Marley made a mental note to frame an enlargement and display it prominently out front.

As she closed the darkroom door, a sardonic smile curled her lips. Always the photographer, never the bride. Would she ever find the hero of her own love story?

Thoughts of Ben ran through her mind. There were so many reasons she shouldn't give in to their attraction—and the fact that he didn't plan to stay in Alpine was the least of them. Ernie had made a valid point yesterday about Ben's apparent issues with God and the church. Marley had struggled too long in her own faith walk to risk involvement with someone whose belief in the Lord wasn't as solid as hers.

But the biggest problem? Getting involved meant eventually having to be honest about her past, because in Marley's book, no relationship could survive for long without complete transparency. She'd seen firsthand how her father's facade of power and success had all but destroyed her parents' marriage.

She'd also witnessed the strength and stability of relationships like that of Healy and Valerie Ferguson, the couple back in Missouri who had mentored her during her last stint in juvenile detention. They'd helped Marley come to terms with her responsibility for the car accident that had injured her friend Tina so badly that she'd been in rehab for months. It was the Fergusons' encouragement and prayers that had gotten Marley through those dark days and made her determined to change.

Yes, Healy and Valerie had the kind of marriage Marley dreamed of, a relationship built on trust, fidelity and unconditional love. But it wouldn't happen until she met the man who would accept her completely—past, present and future.

Maybe it was Ben, maybe not. Only God held the answers. Time to stop daydreaming, gather up her cameras and lighting equipment and get this photo shoot under way.

Twenty minutes later, she was on the road to the Whitlows' ranch. With every mile that passed, her anticipation grew, along with her annoyance over letting a handsome, charming guy like Ben Fisher burrow under her skin so easily.

Around the next bend, Marley glimpsed the broad, wrought-iron ranch gate, the Whitlow name arching over the entrance and bordered by two copper-colored Texas stars. On a whim, she stopped the car outside the gate and reached for her digital camera. Stepping to the gravel shoulder, she snapped several pictures, using the gateposts to frame the rolling pastureland beyond. In one shot, she captured a mare and her foal cavorting in the long grass. Maybe she'd include these photos in a memory album along with the portraits she took of Steve and Jane today.

Back in the Honda, she continued up the lane to the circle drive in front of the ranch house.

As she climbed from the car, Ben appeared on the front porch. "Need any help?"

"Would you grab a couple of the equipment bags from the trunk?" Marley popped the latch, then added with a teasing grin, "Provided you're not too sore from hauling paint buckets and guacamole."

"Yeah, it was the guacamole that did it." Gritting his teeth, he massaged one shoulder. "Maybe I'd better get my wheelchair."

Marley laughed and handed up one of the lighter bags. "Here, I think you can handle this one without hurting yourself."

He set it by the front door and then trotted down the porch steps, meeting Marley behind her car. "Last night was fun. I enjoyed getting to know your friends, especially when Ernie wasn't giving me the third degree."

Cringing, Marley grinned up at him. "Ernie's just a good friend who thinks it's his business to look out for me."

"So I gathered." Ben reached into the trunk

and looped his arm through a bag strap. "Any particular place you want this stuff?"

Marley glanced around. "Why don't we start on the front porch? I really like the view."

"Pretty spectacular, isn't it?" Ben's gaze shifted suddenly from Marley's face to the horizon, and he cleared his throat.

With a self-conscious gulp, she reached for another bag and followed Ben to the porch. "We should probably get started. If you'll bring Steve and Jane out, I'll set up my equipment."

Ben nodded and went inside. In the meantime, Marley arranged her camera tripod and light stands for reflectors. A few minutes later, Ben returned with his aunt and uncle.

"Oh, Marley," Jane gushed, "I've been flighty as a nervous hen all day. Still can't believe we're doing this!"

"You look gorgeous—love the new haircut. Thought we'd start with you two on the porch swing." As the couple moved toward the swing, Marley touched a finger to her lips as she pondered how best to pose them.

Immersed in her work, she easily pushed all other thoughts from her mind. After taking several photos on the front porch, she moved everything inside and staged some shots near the fireplace. When Marley felt she'd captured the best portrait poses, she invited the Whitlows to pretend they were showing a stranger around the ranch, while she continued snapping candid photos of the couple in various settings.

Finishing up outside the barn, Marley shut off her camera and capped the lens. "That should be plenty for me to work with. I'll have proofs ready for you by the end of the week."

"Hang on," Ben interjected. "I've got one more idea for some really good pictures."

Marley narrowed her eyes. "Here we go again, the amateur giving advice to the pro."

"No, seriously. If you really want to capture Uncle Steve and Aunt Jane in their element, you have to get some shots of them on horseback." Ben motioned toward the barn.

Marley turned to Jane with an obliging smile. "It's totally up to you."

Jane shared a glance with her husband. "You know, we could all ride up to the ridge where those fall wildflowers are growing."

"Wait—*ride* out there? On horseback?" Marley shook her head. "I don't ride."

All three of them—Steve, Jane and Ben—stared at her as if she'd grown another head.

Ben raised his brows and blinked. "You've lived in Texas for ten years and you don't ride?"

"That settles it," Steve said. "Today's your first lesson. Ben, help me saddle up Dancer. He'll give our greenhorn the smoothest ride."

Jane clucked her tongue. "Not in your good clothes! We should all go change first. Marley, are you okay riding in those jeans?"

"Uh…" Surely there was a graceful way out of this.

"Now, don't you worry about a thing, honey." Jane offered a reassuring pat to Marley's arm. "Dancer's gentle as a puppy. He'll take real good care of you."

Yes, but puppies were small and cuddly. Horses were…big. Marley forced her mouth into a semblance of a smile. "I should pack up some of my equipment."

And maybe by then they'd forget about putting her on a horse and she could quietly slip away.

One hand on Ben's shoulder, Steve turned toward the barn. "Pour us some sweet tea, hon. We could all use a cool drink before we ride. Be right in soon as I check on Ruby one more time."

Ben caught Marley's eye and mouthed *sorry*, but the laughter in his eyes said he wasn't a bit sorry for wrangling her into a horseback ride.

Nerves tingling, Marley swallowed. "We won't be too long, will we? I have a few things to take care of back in town."

"Not long at all. It's just a short ride out to the ridge." Arm tucked around Marley's waist, Jane guided her across the back lawn. "Honestly, I don't know how you do all you do, sweetie. Manage your studio, teach classes, serve on your church's outreach committee."

"Staying busy keeps me out of trouble." Her light laugh belied the deeper truth to her statement. Too bad she hadn't learned that lesson as a teenager.

In the kitchen, Jane nudged Marley to a chair at the oak table. "Take a load off for a minute while I get the tea. I'm sure glad you're getting Ben involved with the Candelaria ministry. It'll be so good for him. You're going back at Christmas, right?"

"That's the plan." Marley pursed her lips. "I'd hate to think Ben feels any pressure about helping on our committee. Anyway, I'm sure he'll find another job soon."

"If he does, he does." Jane set a glass of tea in front of Marley and lowered her voice. "But between you and me, I'd be mighty happy to see our boy get out of the corporate rat race and settle down right here in Alpine."

Marley couldn't think of an appropriate response, so she gulped some tea. Time to get her camera gear packed and stowed so she could make a quick getaway after she made a complete fool of herself on horseback.

* * *

"She sure looks better than yesterday." Ben reached over the stall gate to scratch Ruby behind the ear. The horse rewarded him with a whinny.

"Couple days' rest and she'll be good as new." Uncle Steve tossed a flake of hay into the next stall for Dancer, a gray gelding with reddish speckles in his coat. "Man, I was glad you drove up yesterday when you did. Couldn't have handled our old girl without you. You're a natural, Ben."

"Natural at doing what I'm told." Ben laughed. "And I do remember how you always bossed Aidan and me around when we came out for summer vacations."

"Hey, you calling me bossy?" Uncle Steve shot Ben a mock glare.

Ben grinned back. "If the boot fits."

"Well, for a couple of self-proclaimed city boys, y'all sure acted like you were having fun."

"Tagging along, helping with the livestock, pretending we were real cowboys? Yeah, it was a lot of fun."

Uncle Steve arched a brow and clapped Ben on the shoulder. "Like I've been saying, country life suits you."

Biting his tongue, Ben shrugged. He couldn't

even pretend he didn't enjoy being at the ranch, and pitching in with ranch chores definitely provided a refreshing change from office work. But it couldn't go on forever. Eventually, Ben needed to return to the real world.

Along with a real paycheck.

After changing into a scruffier pair of jeans and the well-worn hand-me-down boots his uncle had given him a few days ago, Ben caught up with Marley as she carried a few things out to her car. "You're not mad, are you? This'll be fun, I promise."

"The kind of fun where I'll be walking funny for the next week?" She shifted a canvas zipper bag to make room in the trunk for a camera case. "Look, I know I've been merciless with the city-boy stuff. But the truth is, I grew up in a large metropolitan area just like you did. Being around horses and cows and other big hairy beasts isn't exactly in my comfort zone."

The vulnerable look in her eyes tugged at something deep inside Ben's chest. He shook it off and hefted another of her bags into the trunk, then closed the lid. "If it makes you feel any better, I hadn't been on a horse since the last time I came for a visit, which was longer ago than it should have been, so I was walking funny my whole first week in Alpine."

"Uh-huh. I *definitely* feel better now." Marley slanted him a sardonic frown.

Ben laughed. "Come on, let's go introduce you to one of those 'big hairy beasts.'"

In the barn, Uncle Steve already had Dancer in the cross ties. Shifting a black sport saddle higher on the gray gelding's withers, he grinned at Marley. "Our most comfortable tack on the gentlest horse, all for you."

Marley timidly stretched out her hand for Dancer to sniff. "I'm hoping his name isn't any indication of what I can expect on the trail."

Ben and his uncle exchanged grins, and then Ben explained, "He got the name because Aunt Jane says his canter is as smooth as one of those Viennese waltzes they do on *Dancing with the Stars.*"

"Canter?" Marley shuffled backward, right into Ben's chest.

Ben grabbed her by the elbows to help her regain her balance. He covered the awkwardness of the moment with a weak chuckle. Why did she have to be so enchantingly cute? "Don't panic. No cantering until you're ready."

"Let's just keep it at a walk. A *slow* walk. Standing still would be even better."

Aunt Jane came out a few minutes later, and soon they had four horses saddled and ready. With Ben on one side and Uncle Steve on the other, they helped Marley climb onto Dancer's back and adjusted her stirrups. When Ben handed up her camera, she looped the strap over her neck with one hand while gripping the pommel with the other.

"Just be glad you're not riding Prancer," Ben said, nodding toward Uncle Steve's horse, Dancer's nearly identical brother. "He definitely lives up to his name."

With Aunt Jane mounted on Snow, her white Arabian mare, Ben cast Marley another reassuring smile before climbing on Skeeter, a tall Palomino gelding. Uncle Steve took the lead and they set out for the ridge.

The trail led through acres of Whitlow ranch land, a panorama of rolling hills tufted with hardy desert grasses, cacti and a variety of low-growing shrubs and trees. Ben enjoyed watching Marley's death grip on the pommel slowly relax as the spectacular scenery captured her attention.

When they reached the ridge, arrayed in white, gold and purple wildflowers Ben couldn't even begin to name, Marley sighed in wonder. "It's gorgeous. Absolutely gorgeous."

They sat on their horses for several minutes just taking in the view, until Ben nudged Skeeter closer to Marley on Dancer and murmured,

"You're not wearing that camera for decoration, are you?"

Her mouth formed a perfect O before her eyebrows shot up and she gave an embarrassed laugh. After some careful positioning for lighting and background, and with some help from Ben to keep Dancer steady, she snapped several more pictures of Steve and Jane.

All too soon, for Ben, anyway, it was time to head back. With Marley feeling more at ease on horseback, they were able to carry on an actual conversation. It also helped that Aunt Jane got Marley talking about Candelaria again, because Marley could chat nonstop on that subject.

When she brought up the committee's dilemma about trying to come up with an original fund-raising idea, the answer hit Ben so hard that his reflexive action startled Skeeter. When he'd quieted the horse, he rode up beside Marley. "Your committee should sponsor a trail ride. Right here on the ranch. For a minimum donation, people can bring their own horses and enjoy some of the best scenery this side of Alpine."

Marley looked from Ben to his uncle. "Wow. Would that even be possible?"

"We've hosted small trail rides here before," Uncle Steve said. "There'd be a few more things to consider for a big event like you're talking about, but I'd sure be willing to consider it."

Ben could almost see Marley's mind spinning with the possibilities. While they continued on to the barn, she and Uncle Steve traded thoughts on several logistics issues—rider safety and insurance liability were two immediate concerns. Aunt Jane sparked on the idea of having food and entertainment.

"And Ben's got the promotion experience," Uncle Steve said as they dismounted in front of the barn. "Marley, it looks like you've got all the bases covered if you want to go ahead with this."

She looked excited but shell-shocked as Ben took Dancer's reins from her. "We're having another committee meeting after the work team gets back from Candelaria. I'll bring it up then. Should we go over some possible dates?"

The subject of choosing a date hit Ben like a punch to the solar plexus. In his enthusiasm for the idea, he'd conveniently forgotten he probably wouldn't be around long enough to help much. Leading his and Marley's horses into the barn, he left the conversation to the others while he worked on putting away saddles and bridles.

The ladies went inside ahead of Ben and his uncle. They found them sipping tea at the kitchen table.

Aunt Jane gave several sniffs, wrinkling her nose in disgust. "Uh, someone might need to check his shoes."

Uncle Steve grimaced as he inspected his boot soles. "That'd be me. Must have stepped in something in one of the stalls."

While his uncle went outside to remove the offending boots, Ben washed his hands in the guest bathroom. By the time he returned to the kitchen, Marley was saying her goodbyes.

"I'll grab the rest of your gear and walk you out," Ben insisted.

While he stowed two more bags in her trunk, she stretched and groaned.

"Not sorry I talked you into a horseback ride, I hope?" Ben opened her car door for her, taking a moment to appreciate the scent of herbal shampoo mixed with horse smells and fresh air.

"It was great. And I'll never be able to thank you enough for coming up with the trail-ride suggestion." Her brown eyes still sparkled with enthusiasm. "You should come to our next Spirit Outreach meeting and gives us your thoughts about publicity."

He backed off a step. "I might have come on a little strong about that. I mean, I'm glad to do what I can while I'm in town, but…"

"But you don't know when a new job will come through." Marley nodded. "I get it, really."

Just then, Ben's cell phone rang. He doubted it was a job offer on a Sunday evening but figured he'd better check anyway. It was his father, calling from Houston. "Don't leave yet," he told Marley. "This'll just take a sec."

He strode across the circle drive to the grassy area beyond. "Hey, Dad."

"Hey, son. How's it going? You having a good visit with Steve and Jane?"

"Yeah, great." He glanced back at Marley and shot her a quick smile.

"Nothing new on the job front?"

"Nada." Ben grimaced. "But any day now, I'm sure."

"Paula and I keep you in our prayers." A pause, which Ben chose not to fill. Prayer wasn't his thing, at least not since Mom died. "Guess it's too early to know whether you'll be back in Houston for Thanksgiving?"

"That's two months away. Anything could happen."

"Right. Well…" Dad's attempt to keep the conversation going wore thin.

"I should go. We've got company."

"Think about Thanksgiving, though."

Ben promised he would and ended the call. He stifled a sigh and walked back to Marley. "Sorry, it was my dad."

She looked down briefly through lowered

lids. "Fathers. Yep, can't live with 'em, can't live without 'em."

"You say that like you know something about dysfunctional families."

"Every family has problems of one kind or another." She rested her chin on the open door, a warm smile lighting her face. "But this Candelaria outreach has a way of giving you a whole new outlook. It isn't about crying over what you don't have, but being thankful and making the most of what you've got."

Ben ran a palm over the back of his head. "Guess that's one skill I haven't mastered."

"Don't beat yourself up," Marley said with a chuckle. "I'm still working on it, too."

"And obviously doing a lot better job of it than I am." Ben knew he was stalling, but he hated to see the afternoon come to an end. "You sure made Aunt Jane and Uncle Steve's day today. Thanks for doing this."

"The pleasure was all mine. They're great people." Marley straightened. "I should get going."

Ben noticed she didn't seem in any more of a hurry than he was. "You have plans for this evening?"

"I should start going through all these photos, and then..." Her voice trailing off, she gave an apologetic shrug. "Actually, just putting my feet up in front of the TV."

"Sounds exciting." He moved closer, resting his hand solidly on the roof of the car to keep from twining his fingers in her ponytail. "Aunt Jane always cooks for an army. She wouldn't mind if you stayed for supper."

Marley studied him for several long moments. Her mouth firmed. "Tempting as your offer may be, I don't relish being used as a distraction."

"Distraction?" Ben blinked.

"Distraction, dalliance, diversion—pick your *D* word." Her expression softened, along with her tone. "What I'm trying to say is, I'm here in Alpine for the long haul, and—"

"And I'm not." Guilt seared Ben's chest. Allowing this attraction to grow any stronger wasn't fair to either one of them, and yet he couldn't stop himself. "But I enjoy spending time with you, Marley. Can't we just take it day by day and see what happens?"

As she gazed off into the distance, he could see the struggle behind her eyes. Then, when he'd grown certain she was about to call an end to this…whatever it was between them, she stepped away from her car. "Okay, I'll stay. It's just supper with friends, right? And since when have you known me to turn down a free meal?"

***

She shouldn't have stayed. But how could Marley pass up Jane Whitlow's delicious meal of bratwurst, sauerkraut, lima beans with bacon bits and German potato salad? And Dutch apple pie for dessert!

As for spending more time with Ben, well, that was nice, too. So what if he didn't plan to stick around Alpine? She wasn't exactly in the market for a long-term relationship anyway. Not with a business to run and too many mistakes from her past she'd rather keep private, for her own sake as well as her father's.

As Ben walked her out to her car later, the first stars had twinkled into view, the western horizon bathed in shades of deep purple and magenta. His fingertips grazed her arm as he opened her car door, and she shivered. He stood so close she could smell the coffee and cinnamon-spiced apples on his breath.

Here was the real reason she shouldn't have stayed. If she stood here a moment longer, he would surely try to kiss her.

And she would let him.

"Ben…" One hand lightly touching his chest, she eased away. "I really need to go."

He stepped closer, his fingers encircling her wrist. "You doing anything tomorrow?"

"I'll be very busy, actually." She tried to look occupied finding her car keys. "I have all these photos to process, remember?"

"Oh, yeah." He grinned shyly and backed away. "Good night, Marley. It was a fun day."

She offered a weak smile as she climbed in behind the wheel. "Good night, Ben. Tell Jane thanks again for supper. It was fantastic."

The drive into town seemed endless. She tried hard to keep her thoughts on all the ideas they'd talked about for the trail ride, and when that didn't work, she mentally ran through some of the better shots she'd captured of Jane and Steve.

But she kept picturing the mischievous sparkle in Ben's hazel eyes, and the cute way his messy, movie-star hair stood on end when he took off his baseball cap at the end of their horseback ride.

You've got to stop this, Marley. She had her issues, he had his. It was best to keep things at the friendship level before someone got hurt.

Wasn't it?

Chapter Six

The following week kept Marley swamped with activity, which turned out to be a blessing. What with planning lessons and activities for the after-school photography class, wrapping up a travel magazine assignment and selecting the best proofs to show the Whitlows for their anniversary portrait, she had little time to think about Ben.

When Steve and Jane dropped in on Friday, Marley was finishing a phone conversation with Pastor Chris about the ministry team that had just returned from Candelaria. As he described everything the team had accomplished, Marley suffered another twinge of envy that she hadn't been able to go along. She took enough time off from the studio as it was, especially with budget worries mounting, so her next trip would have to wait until the Texas Tech students came down on their Christmas break.

Marley showed the Whitlows to a round table at the back corner of the studio and brought up the proofs on a large computer screen. "I'm going to let you browse at your own pace while I check on something in the darkroom. I'll be back in a few minutes."

Jane was already exclaiming over the shots as Marley slipped down the back hallway. She smiled to herself, knowing the challenge her friends faced.

By the time she rejoined them, they didn't seem any closer to making a decision. Steve drew a hand across his mouth as he stared at the screen. "Wish we could have brought Ben along for his opinion. It's his gift, after all."

The couple shared a look, and against her better judgment, Marley asked, "What's Ben doing today? I admit, I'm surprised he didn't come in with you."

Exhaling sharply, Steve shook his head. "Took off for El Paso early this morning for a job interview."

"That's...good." Marley swallowed. "Isn't it?"

Jane crossed her arms. "I'm praying he doesn't get the job."

"Sweetheart!" Steve stared at his wife. "Much

as we'd both like Ben to stay, we can't go praying against our nephew's success."

"We can if we don't believe it's right for him. He won't be happy there. I know it in my bones."

Marley thought it best to stay out of the discussion. She pulled out a chair and sat next to Jane, then reached for the computer mouse. "Here's one of my favorites from the wildflower ridge."

They eventually narrowed their selection to three poses, but Jane insisted she couldn't possibly decide until Ben cast a vote. "He'll be back late this evening," Jane said. "Will you be in the studio tomorrow, Marley?"

"What if I print out your favorites so you can take the proofs with you? No reason Ben needs to make a special trip into town."

Another curious look passed between Jane and her husband. Jane turned an engaging smile toward Marley. "We shouldn't influence his choice. I'll send him over in the morning first thing."

The Whitlows hurried on their way, as if to ensure Marley wouldn't have the chance to argue.

She needed to talk to Ben anyway to remind him about the next Spirit Outreach meeting, scheduled for Monday evening. They could definitely benefit from his advice about publicity, even if he did find a job and leave soon.

And yet…El Paso was less than a four-hour drive away. Not unreasonable for maintaining a relationship.

Not exactly convenient, either.

Marley *had* to stop thinking like this! Too much stood between her and a romantic future, with Ben or anyone else.

After lunch, Marley worked a while longer in the darkroom, then packaged up a set of color enlargements for the travel magazine editor. Deciding to close the studio early, she headed to the post office and the grocery store. A frozen lasagna entrée and salad were calling her name, along with a rented DVD. Nothing beat curling up on the sofa for a quiet evening at home.

Yes, despite the opinions of her single friends, dating was highly overrated, not to mention stressful and exhausting. The Coutus, Pastor Chris and his wife and several other well-meaning church members had tried more than once to set up Marley with an eligible bachelor—someone who met their incredibly high standards, naturally. But Marley had yet to meet the guy she felt she could be fully herself with, much less spend the rest of their lives together.

Besides, with the fund-raiser to think about now, she had all she could handle.

When she opened the studio just before ten the next morning, she found Ben leaning against a parking meter out front. Her stomach did a tiny flip-flop as she pulled open the door. "Hi. Been waiting long?"

"Just a couple minutes." Thumbs hooked through the belt loops of his jeans, Ben ambled inside. "Aunt Jane sent me over to look at those proofs."

"Sure. I'll bring them up on the computer for you." She motioned him over to the table in the back corner. "So…how was El Paso?"

Ben shrugged and sank into a chair. "Not promising. Probably a wasted trip."

"I'm sorry." Marley hoped her words sounded sincere, because she couldn't suppress a flutter of relief. Best change the subject and show Ben the photos so he could be on his way.

After they'd scrolled through the Whitlows' top three choices several times, Ben blew out a breath through pursed lips. "Aunt Jane isn't sorry."

It took Marley a full five seconds to make the connection to her earlier remark about the job interview. "Did she actually say so?"

"Didn't have to. The four-egg Denver omelet she served me for breakfast said it all."

"Maybe she was just trying to cheer you up."

Ben snickered. "And did I mention she asked what color I'd like them to paint the guest room?"

"You're kidding."

"I wish!"

Nothing subtle about Jane Whitlow. Turning her attention to the computer screen, Marley suppressed a grin. "It's pretty clear she and your uncle would both love for you to stick around Alpine for a while."

"And I've done everything in my power to make it clear that Alpine doesn't fit into my career plans."

Marley cringed inwardly at the finality in his tone. She subtly increased the space between their chairs, and for the next few minutes they silently reviewed the photos, until Ben reached up and tapped the screen. "This is the one."

"I agree. It's been my favorite all along." Marley sat back and admired the shot. It was among the last few she'd taken, a candid shot out on the wildflower ridge snapped when Steve and Jane had forgotten they were being photographed. Their horses side by side, Steve had reached for Jane's hand, and she'd gazed across at him with a look of utter contentment. Marley had been so entranced by the love shining in their eyes that she'd almost missed the shot.

Now, studying the picture, Marley's eyes

welled up. *Dear God, let me know love like that someday.*

"So what's next?" Ben's question startled her out of her reverie.

She flicked a bit of moisture off her cheek. "Now we need to talk about size, canvas, frame—" With a nervous laugh, she continued, "All the stuff you *didn't* want to get into the first time we discussed doing a portrait."

"Ah. You mean the expensive part." Ben leaned forward to tug his wallet from his back pocket. He slapped his American Express card on the table. "As far as I know, this thing still works. My aunt and uncle deserve the best."

"All right, then. I'll get my catalogue and we can write up the order."

By the time Ben made his selections, the cost of a simple anniversary portrait had skyrocketed. As Marley ran his credit card, he clenched his jaw and hoped he landed another job soon.

He pocketed the receipt and thanked Marley again for helping him with the gift. "I can tell you cut me a deal on the sitting fee. Really appreciate it."

With a friendly laugh, she walked him to the door. "Who am I to take advantage of an out-of-work corporate exec?"

"Didn't stop you the day I took you for a steak dinner."

Marley flinched. "Are you ever going to let me forget?"

Her pitiful pout pulled at his insides. A smile crept across his lips before he tore his gaze away and reached for the doorknob. "Let's just call it even—a steak dinner for a portrait sitting."

"Sounds fair to me." Marley followed him as far as the front sidewalk. "I guess you're still sending out résumés?"

Ben watched a mom push a baby stroller past. The dad carried a sippy cup and held an older child's hand. The family looked happy to be out and about on a bright fall day. Must be nice to be so carefree.

Must be nice to have a family.

He returned his attention to Marley. "Résumés. Yeah, still working on those. But even if I snag another interview, hiring decisions take time. I should be around to help with the Candelaria fund-raiser for a few more weeks at least."

"That's great. And trust me, you'll gain a lot more from the experience than you give."

Ben mulled over her words for a moment, then narrowed one eye. "Is that a commentary on my value to the committee?"

"What? No! I just meant—"

"I know what you meant." Ben couldn't help laughing at her sudden look of chagrin.

And then he wasn't laughing anymore because something about Marley Sanders made him all the more conscious of that empty space in his heart he'd been saving for the right woman to fill.

"Pardon me." A white-haired woman in a lime-green sweater came up beside Ben. "Is this your studio?"

"Uh, no, it's this young lady's." Ben nodded toward Marley as he stepped aside. "And believe me, she's really good."

A faint blush crept up Marley's cheeks. She offered her hand. "Hi, I'm Marley Sanders. Are you looking for a photographer?"

"Actually, I'm interested in enrolling my grandson in your children's class. Is it too late?"

"Not at all. Give me one second and I'll be right with you." After showing the woman inside, Marley turned to Ben with a shy smile. "Good luck with the job hunt. Oh, before I forget, can you come to our next outreach committee meeting? It's Monday night."

"Sure, I'll be there. And since I've got all this time on my hands..." He angled her a hopeful glance. "Maybe you could use some help with your class next week?"

Marley's gaze turned doubtful. "You're serious?"

"Why not? I could be your gofer, or model, or—"

She folded her arms and tapped her index fingers on the opposite elbows. The scheming look in her eyes made him nervous. "Okay, you're on. We meet here at the studio Monday through Friday, three thirty to five."

As Ben strolled down the sidewalk to where he'd parked the Mustang, he found himself whistling. What had come over him, anyway? What business did he have volunteering to help with Marley's class when he should be spending every spare minute looking for work?

Because you'd rather spend time with her, and you'll find any excuse to do so.

If that was the case, he'd better make the most of what job-hunting time he had. He climbed in his car and drove several blocks to a coffee shop with Wi-Fi. Cappuccino in hand, he claimed a corner table and powered up his laptop.

But after scrolling through the new job listings and finding nothing of interest, he resorted to aimlessly surfing the internet while his mind kept drifting back to Marley.

Marley had such a heart for the people in

Candelaria. Ben sensed a fire kindling in his belly—an urgency to take action, to somehow make things better. He'd spent his adult life focusing all his attention on getting ahead in the corporate world. To care this much about people he didn't know and who could in no way advance his career goals was a strange new experience for him.

Absently, he sipped his cappuccino, only to sputter when the lukewarm brew hit his tongue. Time to get back to the ranch and help Uncle Steve with the barn repairs this afternoon.

As Ben shut down his computer and slid it into its case, he felt the roughness of new calluses forming on his hands. Helping Uncle Steve at the ranch, unloading supplies for the Candelaria team—how long had it been since he'd expended this much physical effort? Oddly, the tasks he'd taken on since arriving in Alpine seemed to be scraping away a few of the calluses on his heart.

And it felt good.

A full class felt good. And Marley couldn't be prouder of the creative and captivating photos her nine students had produced this past week.

True, some of the credit went to Ben. She never fully believed he'd show up for the first day of class, much less stick it out the entire week. She also never imagined his marketing and promotion experience would turn out to be such an asset to the class. When he suggested the kids try photographing random items as if featuring them in an advertising campaign, it added a whole new dimension to Marley's lesson plans.

"Miss Sanders?" A twelve-year-old girl in overall cutoffs tugged on the hem of Marley's T-shirt. "Are we gonna get our pictures to take home?"

"Absolutely, Jill. Every photo you took this week will go on a DVD that you can view on your computer or TV." Marley nodded toward the back room, where she'd sent Ben to copy the jpeg files from each student's digital photo card to the child's personal DVD. "Mr. Fisher should have those ready by the time you leave today."

Jill smiled her satisfaction as she wandered over to Marley's display wall. "I want to take pictures as good as these someday and be a famous photographer like you."

"Famous? Hardly!" Marley laughed. Relative anonymity suited her just fine. "But I do enjoy my work."

The brass bells clanged as the front door swung open and two moms entered the studio. "Hey, Marley," one of them called, "bet you're ready to see the last of these kids for a while."

"Are you kidding? We've had a great week."

Ben strolled in from the back with a handful of DVDs. "All done. Never seen so many great photos. Marley, you may find yourself facing some stiff competition in the next few years."

The students crowded around him as he called their names and handed out the DVDs. By the time he finished, more parents had arrived. Marley thanked each of them for allowing their children to participate in the class and reminded them she'd be offering another after-school class in January. She didn't mention she might be relocating her studio unless she found a way to cover the rent increase. The reminder that she might be faced with asking her father for more help made her stomach cramp.

When the last kid left, Marley sagged against the counter. It had been a fun but exhausting week. She glanced at Ben as he straightened up the corner table, where Marley had gathered the children for each afternoon's instructional session.

He caught her eye and grinned. "This week turned out to be more fun than I expected. And in case you didn't notice, those kids idolize you."

"I certainly hope not." A sharp exhalation whistled between her teeth. She turned her attention to the student records she needed to file.

"I'm the very *last* person anyone should consider a role model."

Ben appeared beside her, one hand cupping her shoulder. "You're a great photographer and a great teacher, Marley Sanders. Not to mention a great all-around person. Anybody who can keep her cool around nine hyperactive kids for a week while spearheading an outreach fundraiser is definitely someone to be admired."

If you only knew. Marley cast him an awkward smile as she ducked from beneath his arm. "Which reminds me, it looks like we'll have a good turnout at the ranch tomorrow for our meeting to discuss the trail ride."

"Right, the committee's coming out. Uncle Steve's been scouting for the most interesting trail routes. Maybe we could saddle up some horses and—"

"Uh, maybe not. I was sore for almost a week after our last excursion." Marley locked the front door and started turning off lights.

Ben followed her out the back. "You do know the more you use those muscles, the easier it gets."

Kind of like her "independence" muscles from Dad? She already knew her father's opinion of her business management skills. Besides, his handouts always came with strings attached or, at the very least, a lengthy lecture on fiscal responsibility.

At least the kids' class had turned a small profit, and she did have the Stratton-Leonard wedding coming up later this month. She'd covered her September studio expenses with a little bit to spare, and October was starting out reasonably well. She had three more months before the rent increase kicked in, so there was no reason to throw in the towel quite yet.

As they strolled down the alley to the parking lot, Marley thanked Ben once again for his assistance with her class. "Not only was it nice having the extra help, but you gave me some great ideas for the future. The kids really got into the advertising-promotion thing."

"They did, didn't they?" Ben sighed. "Guess my degree isn't a total waste."

Marley paused behind her Honda. "If you can't find a job in retail management, maybe you should consider teaching. Your real-world work experience could be a huge asset."

Ben shook his head. "A week as your assistant was fun. I don't think I'd have the patience to teach full time."

"Maybe not middle schoolers—they can be a handful for any teacher—but I bet you'd do fine at the high school level or even college."

"Maybe." The Mustang beeped as Ben pressed the button on his key fob.

"I'm serious, Ben. You should check with the human resources department at Sul Ross and see if they have any openings."

Ben shrugged. "If nothing else comes up, I'll think about it. Want to get some supper before you head home?"

"Thanks, but Pastor Chris is picking up burgers. A few of us on the outreach committee are having a quick meeting to go over some details before tomorrow." Marley cringed. "I would have asked you to join us, but we won't get into publicity tonight so I didn't want to impose."

"No worries." He pulled open his car door. "Wouldn't hurt to spend the evening zapping a few more résumés into cyberspace."

For a man desperate to find employment, he didn't sound very enthusiastic. Marley climbed into the Civic. "I'm sure any day now your inbox will be overflowing with job offers."

"From your lips to..." His words trailed off, as if he couldn't bring himself to finish the saying.

"To God's ears? Of course I'm praying for you." And she had been, although not always in the way she should have. More like, *Lord, why'd You bring a wonderful guy into my life when there's no chance for anything lasting between us?*

She should really get it out of her head that it was all about her. Maybe God brought Ben to Alpine for other reasons, like to show him there was more to life than working sixty hours a week.

His expression flattening, Ben rested one arm along the roof of the Mustang. "Don't waste your prayers on me. I think God's forgotten I exist."

"Ben..."

He released a heartless laugh. "See you tomorrow at the ranch." He climbed into the Mustang, gunned the engine and drove away.

Marley sat in her car for a full minute before pulling herself together and heading over to Spirit Fellowship. She couldn't get Ben's forlorn expression out of her mind. The signals had been there since the day he'd bought her the steak lunch, when she'd paused to pray over her meal. She had the clear sense that Ben hadn't always been distant from God, and it saddened her to think problems in his life had caused him to believe God didn't care.

All the more reason Candelaria could be part of God's plan for Ben. Maybe he needed to learn that struggle, heartache and loss didn't automatically mean God had turned away, but instead became opportunities to grow in faith and discover new ways to celebrate the Lord's goodness.

Pulling into the empty space next to Ernie's pickup, Marley rested her forehead on her folded hands. *Lord, You know the plans You have for Ben, for me and for this outreach ministry. Let Your will be done.*

Chapter Seven

For Ben, the most difficult part of getting involved with this whole outreach-ministry thing was having to confront his feelings about God. Couldn't he simply do a good thing for a good cause and leave faith out of it?

He had a feeling Marley would disagree.

If he had any sense, he'd put a little professional distance between Marley and him, and concentrate on publicity for this trail ride.

They'd set the date for the Saturday after Thanksgiving, six weeks away. Not a lot of time to organize an event like this, but the locals they hoped would either volunteer or participate were more likely to be free that weekend. Also, the committee had agreed to start small this year. If the ride proved a success, they'd begin planning much earlier next year and build the event into something bigger.

With Uncle Steve, Aunt Jane and six Spirit Outreach committee members, including Marley, gathered around the Whitlows' kitchen table, Ben remained standing, hip propped against the counter.

Aunt Jane shot him a frown. "What are you doing way over there? Grab a folding chair from the hall closet."

"That's okay. I'm not officially on the committee." He flicked a glance toward Marley, but she looked totally engrossed in whatever was on her tablet screen. "Just call me a consultant."

"And we're grateful for your help," Pastor Chris said with a nod. He opened the discussion with the list of organizational responsibilities the committee had come up with. "I'm hoping for plenty of volunteers from within the congregation to help staff the event. We'll need a setup crew, parking attendants, registration coordinator…"

Ben tuned out the rest, making himself useful refilling coffee cups and setting out more of Aunt Jane's mini oatmeal-raisin muffins. The meeting had been in progress for about forty-five minutes when the doorbell rang. Ben went to answer, opening the door to a tall, dark-haired man about his age.

"Hi, I'm Lucas Montero. Marley asked me to come."

"Marley asked you to come?" Ben repeated.

"To the Spirit Outreach meeting? This is the Whitlows', right?"

"Right. Yes. They're in the kitchen. Go on back and I'll grab another chair."

Ben decided maybe he'd take two chairs while he was at it. When he returned to the kitchen, Marley had risen to share a hug with Mr. Tall, Latino and Ruggedly Handsome.

"Lucas, I'm so glad you could make it. I've missed seeing you in church." Marley made room for Ben to set a chair for Lucas next to hers.

"The guide service keeps me pretty busy on weekends." Lucas scooted his chair up to the table. "I try to watch the recorded worship online during the week, though."

Ben yanked open the second chair and squeezed in between Aunt Jane and Judy Jackson, directly across from the late arrival. There was a brief shift in the conversation as Marley quickly filled Lucas in on what they'd discussed so far.

Then she continued, "I thought with your wilderness guide experience you could be available on the trail to point out interesting plants and terrain features."

"Sure, be glad to." Shifting in his seat, Lucas draped an arm around the back of Marley's chair. When he cast her a pearly white grin and she smiled back, Ben looked away.

Pastor Chris turned to him. "Ben, how about sharing some of your publicity ideas before Steve takes us on a tour of the ranch?"

"Uh, sure." Ben reengaged his brain and flipped open the pad where he'd been jotting his notes. "Obviously, the first thing we need to do is get some local media coverage. Ads can get expensive, so I'm thinking public announcements on local radio stations and maybe talking to the features editor at the *Avalanche* about doing a human interest story..." When he glimpsed Marley's furrowed brow and pursed lips, his words trailed off. "Is something wrong?"

Her expression brightened, but not convincingly. "Just taking this all in. Sorry."

It took Ben a beat or two to recapture his train of thought. "As I was saying, I'd also like to see the paper do a story on this committee and the work you're doing in Candelaria." He outlined a few more ideas for advance publicity, then stressed the value of getting media coverage during the actual event. "The more attention you can garner early on, the more ongoing support you can expect from the community at large."

When they'd covered everything, Uncle Steve

invited the group out to the barn, where a couple of his ranch hands had saddled six horses, one for Steve and five for the committee members who'd expressed interest in riding the trail. Pastor Chris, Ernie Coutu and Pete Oldam had asked to ride, along with Ben and Marley.

Then at the last minute Marley changed her mind. "Lucas should go in my place. He needs to get familiar with the trail."

Ben chimed in, "Forget it. Lucas can take my horse. You two go on and enjoy the ride."

Marley smiled uncertainly as she started toward the ranch hand holding Dancer's reins. Then, from somewhere along the main road, a car backfired and the horses jerked their heads up, ears on alert. Even though Dancer's reaction was mild and he settled quickly, Marley didn't look reassured. "I think I'll sit this one out."

No amount of cajoling would get her on the horse, so when it came to a choice between staying behind with Marley or spending the next few hours in the company of Lucas Montero, Ben's decision was easy. Judy Jackson, the retired teacher, said she hadn't ridden since she was a girl but would love the chance to sit on a horse again. One of the hands boosted her into Dancer's saddle and she happily rode off with the group.

While Ben leaned on the fence rail and

watched the riders depart, Aunt Jane invited Marley and Pete's wife, Bonnie, inside for more coffee.

"Be right there," Marley said. She wandered over and stood next to Ben. "Sorry for chickening out."

"Didn't mean to pressure you, but I thought you had a good time when we rode last time."

"I did. But...today felt different." She sighed and rested her forearms on the fence rail.

Several moments of silence elapsed. Ben glanced over, noticing the fatigue lines around her eyes. "You okay?"

"It's been a long week." She lowered her chin onto her folded arms. "And with this trail ride to organize, things are only going to get busier."

"Looks like you'll have plenty of help, though." Ben wanted to ask what she had going with Lucas Montero but decided it was none of his business. Besides, something else was niggling at him. "I couldn't help noticing you looked a little uncomfortable while we were talking about media coverage."

She straightened abruptly and marched a few steps away, then spun to face him. "You're going to keep the publicity local, right? I mean, the plan was to concentrate on the Alpine area, not go for regional or statewide coverage."

"I thought we'd start local, yes. But the further we can spread the word, the more interest we can generate to bring in more aid for Candelaria." Ben cocked his head. "That's the whole point, right?"

"Yes, of course, but—" Marley hesitated briefly before her lips twitched in a tentative smile. "You said *we*."

Surprised at himself, Ben uttered a soft chuckle. "Guess your enthusiasm is rubbing off on me."

Marley glanced over her shoulder to see Jane Whitlow smiling from the kitchen window. Great, she probably thought Marley had stayed out with Ben because they had something going between them. The woman couldn't be sweeter, but she was terrible at disguising her match-making intentions.

With a peek at her watch, Marley started toward the house. "It could be noon before they're back from the ride. There isn't much more I can contribute here, and I desperately need to get some work done at my studio." Something that paid the bills so she could afford to take all this time off for the outreach ministry, keep her studio open *and* get out from under her father's thumb.

Ben fell in step with her. "I thought you'd

want to wait for Lucas to get back. It sounded like you hadn't seen each other in a while."

His tight tone drew her attention. She'd noticed from the moment Lucas arrived that Ben didn't appear to like him much. Which was ridiculous since they obviously didn't know each other. "We see each other at church from time to time. He's a wilderness guide for Purple Sky Expeditions here in Alpine, but he grew up in Candelaria."

"So…you two share a common interest. That's cool."

"It's nice, yes. Lucas drives over to see his family every few weeks, so he delivers any donations we've collected and keeps us posted about what's happening with everyone." Marley paused on the porch. "Remember the photo of the little girl boarding the school bus? That's Isabella, Lucas's niece."

Ben stuffed his fingertips into his jeans pockets. "So…"

Ben couldn't be jealous, could he? Marley arched a brow at him. "Is that *so* like 'Isn't that interesting?' Or *so* like 'What's the rest of the story?' Because there is none."

"So…I guess I'm getting a little too nosy." Ben dipped his chin and peered up with a boyish grin. "Sorry."

With a wry smile, Marley shook her head. "I have to go."

"Yeah. Duty calls." Ben held the door for her.

She said her goodbyes to Jane and Bonnie, then continued out front to her car.

Ben followed, but this time he didn't try any delay tactics like he'd done the day of the Whitlows' photo shoot. He halted on the porch steps and called, "See you at the meeting Monday night?"

"I'll be there."

Before pulling away, she tugged her cell phone from her purse to turn on the ringer and check for messages. A text from her father read Call me ASAP. The time stamp was nearly two hours ago, while she'd had her phone silenced during the meeting. And Dad hated to be kept waiting.

She made him wait another five minutes while she drove down the lane to the Whitlows' entrance gate. Pulling off to the side, she parked and pressed the callback button.

"Where have you been?" her father practically shouted.

"Hi, Dad, nice to talk to you, too."

"Don't get sarcastic with me. I've been calling your studio number all morning. What were you thinking, staying closed on a Saturday?" Dad huffed. "This is no way to run a business, Marsha."

"Marley. *Marley*." She ground her teeth. "I've told you before, Dad. The studio isn't like a retail business. Most of my work is done by appointment."

"Yes, but—" He made a growling noise in his throat. "I didn't call to lecture you about good business practices. I assume you know I'm up for reelection in November."

Forcing politeness into her tone, she asked, "How's the campaign going?"

"Exceedingly well." A meaningful pause. "Which is why I don't need any surprises."

Meaning any reports surfacing about his problem child. A sigh raked her lungs. "Dad, it's been over ten years. Have I done anything to embarrass you since you swept me and my past under the rug?"

"Marsha..."

She didn't correct him this time. It was pointless, anyway, because in her father's eyes she'd always be Marsha Sanderson, juvenile delinquent, and the skeleton in Harold Sanderson's closet he never wanted exposed to public scrutiny.

"Just promise me," her father said tiredly.

Tears welled in her eyes, but she refused to shed them. "You have absolutely nothing to worry about. I wouldn't dream of raining on your victory parade."

"Good. That's good. Now, how's the money situation? Are your bills covered this month?"

"I'm flush." Close enough, anyway, that she was adamant she wouldn't ask her father for another advance. "Dad, I have to go. I'm on my way to the studio right now."

"Very well. Just remember what I said."

"No surprises. Got it."

He paused. "Your mother sends her love."

But there was no "And I do, too." That would be too much to expect from her father. "Love to Mom. Goodbye, Dad."

Marley tossed her phone into the passenger seat and turned onto the road toward town. To get her mind off her dysfunctional family, she reviewed that morning's planning session. They'd accomplished a lot in a short time, and her hopes for a successful fund-raiser continued to grow.

Of course, if not for Ben, they might never have come up with the idea for a trail ride. Thoughts of him brought a smile to her lips. The annoyingly cute city boy certainly was full of surprises.

Marley's stomach clenched as she pulled into her parking spot down the alley from the studio. She really needed to make sure Ben didn't carry his publicity efforts beyond Alpine—or if he did, he kept her name out of it. The chances of anyone making the connection between Marley Sanders and the former Marsha Sanderson were slim, but it wasn't worth taking the risk.

As the event date neared, the Spirit Outreach committee began holding more frequent meetings. With plans to serve cold drinks and burgers after the ride, they had arranged to rent or borrow picnic tables, chairs and a large party tent. A local country-and-western band would provide entertainment.

Marley had already heard several announcements about the trail ride on local radio stations, and Neil Ingram, a feature writer for the *Alpine Avalanche*, offered coverage in a series of articles about Spirit Outreach and their work in Candelaria. With the addition of an information and sign-up page to the church's website, rider registrations were already coming in.

At a committee meeting near the end of October, Pastor Chris summarized their progress to date. "As of this morning, we have twenty-two riders signed up. Most of our supplies have been donated or offered at a reduced rate, but we're still only looking at a profit of around twelve hundred dollars."

Marley's stomach sank. She'd been hoping for at least two or three times that much. "The ride is still a month away. Surely we'll get a few more by then." She knew firsthand from her photography classes about last-minute registrations.

Seated across the table from her, Ben cast a frown in her direction. "Marley, I know you've wanted to keep this local, but Alpine isn't that big a town. We need to widen our reach, and we need to do it now so potential riders can make plans."

She should be happy Ben had obviously grown more invested in the fund-raising event than he'd initially intended. But now she had to weigh her concerns about personal privacy against Spirit Outreach's goals.

Shifting higher in her chair, she jiggled her empty soda can on the tabletop. "Maybe Thanksgiving weekend wasn't such a great idea, after all."

"We can't change it now," Pastor Chris stated. "Ben's right. Let's get the word out in Marfa, Fort Davis, Presidio, Fort Stockton—any town within a hundred-mile radius."

With the rest of the committee in agreement, Marley couldn't argue. She listened and took

132 Rancher for the Holidays

notes during the rest of the meeting, relieved when they finally broke up around ten thirty.

Ben caught up with her as she walked out to the parking lot. "Long night."

"We had a lot to cover." Stifling a yawn, Marley dug through her purse for her keys.

"I hope I didn't step on your toes with the publicity thing, but I know how badly you want this event to succeed."

"No, you're right. We need to get the word out." She unlocked her car and set her purse and tablet computer inside.

Ben didn't seem in any hurry to head to his own car, on the other side of the lot. Marley noticed he tended to park his cute red Mustang well away from other vehicles. He rested an arm along the top of her door, which stood open between them. "Seen much of your friend Lucas lately?"

She cast him an odd look. "Not really. Why?"

"Just asking. I haven't seen much of you except at these meetings, so I wondered where you've been keeping yourself."

"Trying to make a living. What else?" She regretted her tart tone the moment the words left her mouth. "I'm sorry, Ben. That sounded terrible. I should be asking you how the job search is going."

He sagged against the car door. "Going nowhere fast. Which is why I'm glad to have this trail-ride stuff to keep me occupied. Plus Uncle Steve never has any problem coming up with chores for me around the ranch."

"From what I've seen, it looks like you're enjoying your time at the ranch. Have you ever thought about staying, maybe working for your uncle?"

Something between a groan and a laugh rumbled in Ben's chest. "How much did Uncle Steve pay you to say that?"

"I promise, not a cent." Marley couldn't suppress a laugh of her own. "I take it he's made the offer?"

Ben's mouth twisted. "More than once. I keep telling him it'd never work."

Or did Ben simply not want to admit it might? Another yawn crept up on her. "I should get home."

"Right." With a quick breath, Ben cleared his throat and stuffed his hands into his pockets. "So, uh, what's on your schedule this week? Besides the studio and the trail-ride stuff."

She mentally flipped through her calendar. "I'm finishing up a magazine assignment, and this weekend I'm covering a rehearsal dinner and wedding."

"Sounds fun. Uh, you wouldn't possibly be in the market for an assistant, would you?"

"Not in the budget." Marley arched a brow. "Wait. Don't tell me you're volunteering— again?"

"Might be."

She studied him, unsure whether he was serious or just being nice. Then her gaze slipped to his quirky grin and a tingly feeling tickled her insides. She should give him a quick "thanks, but no thanks" right now and be on her way, but her mouth wouldn't cooperate. "Okay, sure," she heard herself saying. "Meet me at the studio Friday afternoon at four."

Playing photographer's assistant for the Stratton-Leonard rehearsal dinner and wedding gave Ben a whole new appreciation for Marley's talents. She didn't require all the extra stands and lighting equipment she'd brought out to the ranch to photograph Uncle Steve and Aunt Jane, but Ben ended up toting three different camera bags full of fancy lenses and flash attachments.

The hardest part, which Marley handled with the utmost tact, was corralling the bride, groom, their twelve attendants, the minister and two huge extended families for a variety of individual and group poses, plus lots of candid shots during the rehearsal dinner and wedding reception.

With music, dancing and a three-course sit-down dinner at the reception, it was close to midnight before the bride and groom departed and the party broke up. The bride's aunt made sure Marley left with several containers of leftovers and offered some to Ben as well, but he declined except for two hefty slices of cake to take home for Aunt Jane and Uncle Steve.

Ben had driven them to the wedding in the Mustang. He pulled up next to Marley's Honda in the parking lot near the studio. "I could fall asleep right here. That was exhausting."

Marley felt around the floorboard for the shoes she'd kicked off the moment she got in the car. "Having your help made my job tons easier. I can't thank you enough."

"It's always fun watching you at work." Ben gave her hand a quick squeeze. "You're good, Marley. Really good."

Even in the darkened car, he glimpsed the uncertainty in her crooked smile. "I love what I do, but…" She straightened, as if shaking off an unpleasant thought. Her smile widened. "Thank you. It's nice to be appreciated."

He had a feeling this wasn't the time to probe her emotions. They were both dead tired, which meant Marley was vulnerable, and so was he. Clearing his throat, he opened his door. "Let's get your gear unloaded so you can head home and get some sleep."

Marley unlocked the back door of the studio and after they stowed her camera equipment, Ben walked her back to the parking lot. As she climbed into her Honda, he thought how natural it would be to give her a good-night kiss on the cheek. Except lately he couldn't seem to shake the idea that he'd like to get to know Marley as more than a friend. And since he didn't know how much longer he'd be in Alpine—

"Got any plans for tomorrow?" Ben blurted out.

Looking up from buckling her seat belt, Marley covered a yawn. "Sleeping in is my number-one priority. I'll probably go to the late service at church, then chill out for the rest of the day."

"You want to chill out at the ranch? Maybe try another ride on Dancer?" When she hesitated, Ben offered a persuasive grin. "Just you and me. No rowdy committee members bouncing around and getting the horses all tense."

She wrinkled her nose. "Can you guarantee there won't be any cars backfiring or other scary noises?"

"Hey, there are no guarantees in life." He tapped the hood of Marley's car. "At least think about it. If you feel like coming out, great. If you decide you'd rather not ride, we'll watch TV or something. Like you said, just chill."

Marley sighed and quirked her lips. "I'll let you know. Right now, I'm too tired to think straight."

Watching her drive away, Ben suspected he wouldn't see her again until the next Spirit Outreach meeting on Monday night.

She surprised him by showing up at the ranch shortly after two on Sunday afternoon.

He leaned against the door frame, enjoying the shy glimmer in her eyes as she stood on the front porch. She looked amazing in a Sul Ross State University sweatshirt, jeans and sneakers, and he couldn't suppress a grin. "Nice to see you looking a little less bleary-eyed."

"I could say the same about you." Marley poked her hands into her back pockets. "I was thinking I'd really like to see the wildflower ridge again. Is your offer for that ride still open?"

Warmth spread through Ben's chest. His grin widened. "Thought you'd never ask."

Twenty minutes later, Ben gave Marley a boost into Dancer's saddle, then climbed on Skeeter, the Palomino he usually rode. Marley showed the same nervousness as her first time on Dancer, but with the horse's calm nature and steady gait, it took her even less time to relax and enjoy the scenery.

The ride gave Ben a chance to show Marley

the trail he and Uncle Steve had been working on to clear away overgrowth, fill holes and smooth over gullies. "We've added two or three more miles since the committee rode the trail. Lots of great photo ops, too, which you'll appreciate. You should have brought your camera."

"What makes you think I didn't?" Marley winked as she tugged a compact digital camera from the pocket of her sweatshirt. "This little baby is my favorite tool for when I can't haul a bunch of camera equipment along and want to be prepared."

"Should have known." Laughter bubbled up from Ben's chest. He still had his mouth open when Marley turned the camera on him and snapped several pictures. "Hey! Give a guy some warning."

"What makes you think I was taking your picture? There's a really cute cow behind you."

Ben swung to look over his shoulder. There was indeed a herd of cattle on the other side of a barbed-wire fence, but none close enough to be discernibly cute.

Marley chuckled. "Gotcha."

"Funny, Sanders. Very funny." Ben held out his hand. "Here, let me snap some shots of you."

She drew her lower lip between her teeth and shook her head. "Oh, no, that's okay."

"What, you don't trust me with your fancy little camera? It has an automatic mode, right?"

"Yes, but…I'm not used to being on the other side of the lens."

"Then it's about time." Ben kept his hand steady until Marley reluctantly changed some settings on the camera and laid it in his palm. While he centered her in the display, she struck a pose and an artificial smile. "Oh, come on, be natural."

Ben kept up a teasing banter while he snapped several pictures. With each one, Marley grew more at ease, but it took her almost as long to get comfortable having her photo taken as it had to relax on Dancer's back.

"Now for a selfie." Ben guided Skeeter close beside Dancer and held the camera facing them at arm's length. He stretched one arm toward Marley to get her to lean closer, then pressed the shutter.

"Okay, you've had your fun." Marley grabbed the camera and switched it to display mode. "Let me see how many of these I'm going to delete."

He was afraid she'd start deleting before he got a chance to look, but her finger slowed as she browsed through the shots. Something changed in her expression, a kind of wistful sadness filling her eyes. Her chest rose and fell as if she held back tears.

Ben touched her arm. "Marley?"

"It's just weird seeing pictures of myself. Even when I was a kid—" She forced a laugh. "Never mind. I'm being silly."

"Wait, what were you about to say about being a kid?"

"Nothing." She turned off the camera and shoved it into her pocket. "Hey, don't you have more trail to show me?"

They rode for another hour before circling back, both working to keep the conversation light. But Ben couldn't shake the growing sense that Marley carried a lot of baggage from a difficult past. He wondered if she'd ever trust him enough to share it with him.

Chapter Eight

The weeks leading up to Thanksgiving kept Marley too busy to think about much besides work and the Spirit Outreach fund-raiser. Just as well, because after letting Ben see her get teary-eyed over a few photos of herself, she needed to regain some perspective. She liked Ben. A lot. But enough to trust him with her past? Not when she hadn't even found the courage to confide in her closest church friends. Besides, any day now, Ben could land a new job and move on.

As they had for the past few years, Ernie and Angela invited Marley to spend Thanksgiving with them. Angela's parents and an older brother and his family arrived from out of town, so the Coutus' dining room table was full. Everyone gorged on turkey with all the trimmings, then napped in front of the TV while occasionally rousing long enough to cheer for their favorite football team.

Friday morning dawned mild and sunny, a perfect day for the nearly twenty volunteers who met at the Whitlow ranch to begin setting up for Saturday's trail ride and cookout. They arranged tables and chairs under the party tent beside the barn, with a flatbed trailer serving as the stage for the band. Steve Whitlow had designated the pasture across from the house to be used for trailer parking. Tomorrow was predicted to be sunny and mild, a gorgeous day for the event, and with the publicity Ben had secured in a variety of West Texas news outlets, rider registrations had almost tripled.

At least the extra coverage hadn't brought any unwanted attention on Marley. Her father's re-election had gone without a hitch, and Missouri State Representative Harold Sanderson would serve another term.

As Marley and Judy Jackson tested power connections in the stage area, Steve Whitlow's red four-wheeler pulled up beside the tent. Ben climbed off the back and strode over. "You ladies need any help?"

"Almost done," Marley said. "How's the trail looking?"

"Ready to ride. Uncle Steve and I just drove the whole length of it to make sure all the trail markers are in place." He whipped off his ball cap and drew his denim shirtsleeve across his forehead. "I need something cold to rinse the dust from my throat. Can I bring y'all anything?"

Judy tipped her head at Marley. "You two go on. I'll finish up here."

Marley had been up since dawn and was more than ready for a break. She walked with Ben to the Whitlows' back porch and sank onto a deck chair while Ben dug through a cooler filled with ice and canned drinks. "I'll take a diet soda if you can find one."

He handed her a frosty can and popped the top on a root beer for himself, then collapsed into the chair next to hers and gazed off toward the activity around the party tent. "Tomorrow's the big day, huh?"

"Can't believe it's finally here." She offered Ben a heartfelt smile. "In case I haven't said it often enough, thank you. Your promotion expertise made all the difference, I'm sure."

"Pshaw, little lady," he said in his pathetically fake John Wayne drawl. "Weren't nothin' at all."

They sipped their drinks in comfortable silence for a few minutes. "How was your Thanksgiving?" Marley asked.

"Quiet and lazy. Naturally, Aunt Jane cooked up way too much food for the three of us."

Marley studied him. Careful to keep her tone casual, she said, "I thought maybe some of your family from Houston might come out."

The grimace on his face told her she shouldn't have brought it up. "Let's just say the family situation is a bit touchy these days." He glanced her way. "You have a nice day with the Coutus?"

"Very." He didn't want to talk about his family, she didn't want to talk about hers. Time to get back to the business at hand. Finishing her drink, she tossed the can in a plastic recycling tub. "I need to find my checklist so we can wrap things up. Tomorrow's going to be a long day."

As Marley crossed the gravel drive on her way back to the tent, a silver pickup drove up. Neil Ingram, the feature writer who'd been covering the event for the *Alpine Avalanche*, signaled to Marley. "Got time for a quick interview? I'd like some feedback from you and a few other volunteers so I can get a head start on my article for Sunday's edition."

"Sure." Marley described some of the tasks the set-up crew had been working on, then gave Neil a chance to talk with Pastor Chris, Ernie and Judy.

When Neil finished with his questions, he snapped a few photos of the crew at work and said he'd be back tomorrow to get shots during the event. "I imagine you'll be taking photos, too, Marley. If you send me some I can use, you'll get the paper's standard freelance rate."

"I'll keep that in mind. Thanks, Neil." Any amount would help to keep the studio afloat. The January rent increase loomed large in her thoughts. Her constant prayer was to make enough profit not only to stay open in her current location, but also to end the emotional tug-of-war with her father once and for all.

Late Saturday afternoon, Ben leaned against the porch rail and looked out across rows and rows of pickups, SUVs and horse trailers. Most of the riders had returned by now and were unsaddling their horses and packing up tack. Ben would have enjoyed heading out on the trail himself, but between directing traffic and taking his turn in the barbecue trailer flipping burgers and grilling brats, he'd had plenty to keep him busy right here.

Music from the country-and-western band drifted his way from the party tent. The trail ride had proven a huge success, and last time Ben had seen Marley and her Spirit Outreach friends, they were toasting each other with soft drinks and sharing a lively discussion about what they could do to make next year's event even better.

Ben almost felt sorry he wouldn't be around to see it.

Aunt Jane came out with another tray of brownies for the concession counter. "What are you doing here all by your lonesome?"

"Just taking it all in. Quite a day, huh?"

"With all the money they raised, looks like it's going to be a wonderful Christmas for Candelaria." Aunt Jane handed him a brownie. "And did you meet the man from Big Bend Assistance Alliance? Marley told me BBAA's making a sizable contribution to Spirit Outreach."

"That's great."

"I hear BBAA might even open a branch office in Alpine." Aunt Jane slanted him a look. "Wouldn't that be nice?"

"Mmm." Ben bit off a chunk of brownie.

In an obvious stalling tactic, Ben's aunt tucked the plastic wrap around the edge of her tray. "You should think about going down with them."

Now he wasn't following her. "What—you mean to Candelaria?"

Her smile spread. "It would be so good for you."

Good for him. Right. "You know I'm taking things one day at a time. Any day now—"

"Yes, yes, I know." Aunt Jane groaned. "You're

starting to sound like a broken record with all this job-hunting rigmarole."

"But I—"

His aunt seized his hand and shoved the rest of his brownie into his mouth, silencing him. "God will provide the right job for you when He's good and ready. And maybe a change of attitude, to boot." With a saucy twist to her blue-jeaned hips, she marched off the porch and across to the tent.

Ben tried not to choke on the brownie. He hadn't tasted brownies as good as Aunt Jane's since his mother was alive. Mom's sudden death had pretty much sealed his opinions about God, too. He probably did need a change of attitude, but it was nothing the right job offer wouldn't fix. And no matter how much coaxing and cajoling Uncle Steve and Aunt Jane dished out, he simply couldn't picture himself living and working on the ranch for the rest of his days. He knew little enough about horses and even less about cattle.

Before he got chocolate frosting all over his jeans, he went inside to wash his hands. As he tore off a paper towel, Marley entered the kitchen with a dishpan full of used serving utensils. He reached across the counter to take it from her. "How's it going out there?"

"The last of the riders just came in and got

some chow. We're about to shut down the serving line." Marley cast a longing gaze toward one of the kitchen chairs.

"Sit down, for crying out loud. You've been running yourself ragged all day." Ben filled a tumbler with ice water from the fridge and gave it to her. They both took chairs. "Have you had a chance to eat?"

"I nibbled here and there." Her fatigue couldn't hide a satisfied glow. "We did good today, Ben. Really good. Those kids are going to have the best Christmas ever."

A gnawing emptiness settled in his belly. When the time came to move on, he'd miss the deep-down satisfaction his involvement with Spirit Outreach had brought. The work had become more than a passing interest or a way to keep busy while he didn't have anything better to do. In a few weeks' time his concern had strengthened even more for Marley's little border town and the people who didn't share his advantages in life.

Marley's hand rested on the table near her water glass. Slowly, Ben slid his hand closer until their fingertips touched. Keeping his eyes lowered, he studied the swirling wood grain in the tabletop. "I was thinking, if I'm still around when your team goes to Candelaria, do you think I could tag along?"

Her quick intake of breath spoke her surprise.

"I'd make myself useful." Glancing up to gauge her expression, he chuckled softly. "You should know by now I can take direction and work well with others."

She raked him with an appraising stare, but humor lit her eyes. "I must say, Mr. Fisher, your résumé is impeccable."

"So am I hired?"

Growing serious, she asked, "Are you sure, Ben? Because I promise you, a trip to Candelaria will change your life, whether you want it to or not."

He drew his fingers into a fist, knuckles resting uneasily on the table as his doubts kicked into high gear. "Like I said, it all depends on if I'm still around at Christmas."

On Monday evening, the Spirit Outreach committee met to review income and expenses from the trail ride and assess the event's overall success. Marley noticed Ben was conspicuously absent. True, his part was finished, but Marley had hoped he'd care enough to share in the glow of what they'd achieved. Guess she'd misread his interest in getting more involved. Obviously, Ben only cared about what was in it for him. Hadn't she nailed it the day he'd asked her to stay for supper after the Whitlows' anniversary photo shoot? A distraction. That's all she, Spirit Outreach and Candelaria meant to him.

When Pastor Chris quoted their net profit from the trail ride, everyone applauded. "So now we need to go shopping," he stated. "Angela, you've got the list of children's names and ages, right?"

"I do." Angela opened a folder and took out several printed pages. "Lucas Montero brought an updated list when he came for the trail ride. I thought we could divide into teams of two and split up the names for buying gifts."

Pastor Chris agreed, and the committee members started pairing off. Marley expected either Angela or Judy would partner with her, but then Angela decided she and Ernie would shop together, and Judy and Pastor Chris teamed up. Since there was an odd number at the meeting, Marley found herself left out.

With a regretful smile, Angela whispered to Marley, "I thought maybe you and Ben…"

Marley shook her head. "Not a good idea. It's okay. I don't mind shopping by myself."

"Why don't you at least ask him? He's one of the team now, after all."

Surely Angela had noticed he hadn't come to tonight's meeting—or was she jumping on the matchmaking bandwagon along with Jane

Whitlow? "I'll think about it. Do you have a list of names for me?"

Angela winked and handed her one of the printouts. "Saved this one especially for you."

Scanning the list, Marley read Isabella's name and warmth rippled through her. Oh, yes, she'd have to find an extra-special Christmas gift for one of her favorite Candelaria children.

The meeting broke up, and Marley gathered her things. Settling into her car, she remembered to turn her phone off silent mode and discovered a voice mail waiting.

It was from Ben. *"Sorry I missed the meeting. A heifer got caught in the fence, and I had to help get her untangled. Then the vet came out to stitch up her leg, and—well, you don't want to hear all this. Anyway, congratulations again on a great fund-raiser."* He paused, as if unsure, then continued. *"Call me sometime, okay? Uh, bye."*

What *was* it about the man, surprising her at every turn? Her heart flip-flopped, and before she could count off all the reasons she should *not* call him back, she hit Redial.

He answered on the first ring. "Hey. How'd the meeting go?"

"Fine. Everybody's thrilled with how well the ride went. I—that is, everyone missed you."

Way to put your foot in it, Sanders. "How's the cow?"

"A little worse for wear, but she'll heal. I, on the other hand, may never again walk without a limp."

"Oh, no! What happened?"

"The heifer wasn't real happy about the vet's big needle, so while I was helping to hold her still, my foot kind of got in the way of her hoof."

"Ouch. Is anything broken?"

"Don't think so, just bruised. I'm propped on the sofa with an icepack on my big toe." The snickering in the background sounded like Ben's aunt and uncle. He snorted. "You can tell what kind of sympathy I'm getting around here."

Marley couldn't help feeling a little sorry for him, herself. "How long before you'll be up and around again?"

"Unless gangrene sets in and they have to amputate, I should be fine in a couple of days."

"Glad to know it's not serious." The urge to laugh nearly choked Marley. She cleared her throat. "So, um, one of the things you missed at the meeting was dividing up a list of kids' names for buying Christmas gifts." She couldn't believe she was really going to ask this. "Any chance you'd like to be my shopping partner? That is, if you think you'll be up to traipsing around a few stores later this week."

As his silence stretched longer, she held her breath. At last, his tone low and earnest, he replied, "Yeah, I'd like that. Thanks for asking."

With another wedding on the schedule for the upcoming weekend, Marley decided Thursday morning would be her best time to close the studio for a shopping trip *and* give Ben's toe a chance to heal. Ben planned to pick her up at the studio around nine thirty, so she arrived an hour early to take care of a few things in her office.

Checking her email, she found another reminder from her landlord about the January rent increase and her stomach bottomed out. Seconds later, a racket started up out front. Then her phone rang. She snatched it up and hoped the caller could hear her over all the noise. "Photography by Marley Sanders."

"Hi, it's Janet next door." Janet Harders owned the antiques shop in the adjoining building, also leased from Marley's landlord. "Guess you can tell they're starting the renovations this morning."

"Seriously? This close to Christmas?" Marley carried the phone to the front window. A construction van had parked crosswise across two spaces, and workmen in gray jumpsuits were unloading ladders and toolboxes.

"Hopefully this won't last long," Janet said.

"Although I have to agree, a face-lift on these old buildings is long overdue."

"Yes, but—" A ladder crashed against the outer wall and Marley flinched. "I'm not sure I can afford the higher rent."

"Please don't say you're moving out. We've been so good for each other's business."

It was true, they often referred drop-ins looking for recommendations, but generally, shoppers were more interested in Janet's antiques and specialty gifts than portrait photography or artistic photo prints. Marley stifled a sigh. "I'm taking it one day at a time. Oh, before I forget, I'll be out of town week after next for the Candelaria trip. Would you mind keeping an eye on things here?"

"Glad to." Janet asked about the fund-raiser, and while Marley tried to tell her about it over the noise from the sidewalk, Ben drove up in his Mustang.

He parked several spaces down from the construction van, then had to duck around one of the ladders on his way to Marley's front door. He shot her a raised-eyebrow look through the glass before stepping inside.

Finishing her call with Janet, Marley carried the phone back to her office and motioned Ben to follow. "I'll be ready to leave in a few minutes," she said, taking her seat at the desk. "There's coffee in the back room if you want some."

"Had plenty already." Ben nodded toward the front. "What's all that about?"

Marley told him about the renovations. "I may not be around long enough to enjoy them, though. Our landlord's raising the rent."

"But you have such a great location here, and in the business world—"

"I know, I know. Location is everything." Not in the mood to have this discussion right now, Marley returned her attention to the computer screen. "Give me a sec to respond to a couple of emails and we can go."

She'd barely typed five words when the phone rang again. It was the mother of the bride whose wedding Marley would be photographing on Saturday. "I'm so sorry to cancel at the last minute," the woman said, her voice shaking, "but Lori's fiancé called off the engagement."

"Oh, no. Are you sure it isn't just prewedding nerves?"

"Absolutely certain." A hardness entered the woman's voice, suggesting there was much, much more to the story. "I'll mail you a check for your cancellation fee. Again, I'm very sorry to have inconvenienced you."

"It's all right, really. Just give my best to Lori." Marley felt horrible for the jilted bride, but as she returned the phone to its cradle, her immediate thought was how she'd been counting on the money from this wedding to get her through the rest of December. Stomach churning, she sat back and closed her eyes.

"Marley?" Ben's gentle tone reminded her they still had a shopping date.

"We should get going," she said, pushing up from the chair. Then she immediately collapsed again as the combination of worry, frustration and anger drained the strength from her knees.

Ben rounded the desk and sank to one knee beside her. "Something tells me this isn't only about a photo gig getting canceled. Want to talk about it?"

She waved a hand. "Not really." It would be too difficult to describe her financial concerns without letting something slip about how—and why—her father subsidized the business. "It'll all work out...somehow. God hasn't let me down yet."

The instant she spoke the words, it was like watching a curtain fall across Ben's face. He stood slowly, putting distance between them. "I wish I had your faith."

His defeatist expression squeezed Marley's heart. She might be struggling to cover expenses, but at least she knew God was on her side. "Give Him a chance, Ben. God always has a better plan than anything we can devise on our own."

It was a truth she desperately needed to hold on to for herself.

"We'll see," Ben muttered. Straightening, he glanced at his watch. With a forced smile, he suggested they head out on their shopping trip. "I hope you're better at picking out kids' gifts than I am. My only experience is for my twin nephews, and they're easy to please with video games."

Thoughts of the children lifted Marley's spirits. Rising, she snatched her purse from the corner of the desk. They exited through the front door, and as Marley locked up, she gave herself a mental talking-to. If the people of Candelaria, as little as they had, could remain hopeful, she could, too.

Now, if only she could rekindle a spark of that hope in Ben. As far as she knew, he still planned to go along on the mission trip. She wasn't sure how it would happen, but something told Marley his experience in Candelaria might be the key to restoring his faith.

Chapter Nine

"Got my toothbrush, shaving supplies, extra pair of sneakers..." Ben was more than a little amazed at himself for actually going through with the Candelaria trip, but still jobless and with no prospects on the horizon, he'd run out of excuses to back out. Brows scrunched together, he tossed a duffel bag into the backseat of his uncle's pickup. "Guess this is it. Hope I didn't forget anything."

Uncle Steve climbed in behind the wheel. "If you did, somebody'll have something you can borrow. They keep the reimbursement store pretty well stocked, too."

Ben pictured the little red barn in Marley's photograph and wondered if the store carried his favorite brand of ice cream.

Probably not.

Aunt Jane came around to Ben's side of the

pickup. "Don't forget to deliver the little gift I'm sending along."

"Packed it right on top. No worries."

Gripping Ben's face between her palms, Aunt Jane planted a noisy kiss on his cheek, then wrapped him in a hug. "So glad you're doing this. It'll be the experience of a lifetime."

Ben had no doubt she was right, but her enthusiasm didn't lessen his discomfort. "You keep Uncle Steve in line while I'm gone. And don't forget to check my email." Although he had few hopes of employment news during a holiday month.

Aunt Jane patted Ben on the backside and nudged him into the pickup. "Have a little faith, honey. God'll work it all out."

Ben kept his smile in place as he pulled the door shut and waved through the window. He'd definitely gotten an earful about faith since coming to Alpine. Not that he hadn't felt the pressure from his dad and brother back in Houston, but Ben wasn't sure he knew what faith was anymore.

The first fingers of dawn had just crept over the horizon when Uncle Steve pulled into the Spirit Fellowship parking lot. Marley, Ernie and Pastor Chris stood in a circle with the college students from Texas Tech, heads bowed and holding hands.

"Go on over," Uncle Steve said as he shut off the engine. "I'll bring your things."

"That's okay. Wouldn't want to interrupt."

Too late. Marley caught his eye through the windshield and signaled him over. Pulling air into his lungs, Ben stepped from the pickup and strode to Marley's side. She made room for him to join the circle and took his hand. He tensed at her touch, then folded his fingers around hers.

Pastor Chris, standing on Marley's other side, leaned forward. "Everybody, this is Marley's friend Ben Fisher. He helped a lot with our fund-raiser event, so we're glad it worked out for him to join us on the trip."

Murmured greetings traveled the circle and Ben nodded in response. Why a bunch of college kids should make him so nervous, he had no idea.

"We were just about to pray over the trip." Pastor Chris cleared his throat and lowered his head.

Ben was surrounded by people who believed in a God who cared. Something shifted in his gut as Pastor Chris began his prayer.

"Dear Lord, we ask Your blessing on this journey. You've given us work to do and hands to do it, and we pray for the strength, wisdom and courage to do Your will. As we take this journey together in faith, let Your Holy Spirit speak into each person's heart the lesson You would have us learn from the experience. For we pray in Jesus's name. Amen."

"Amen," Marley whispered, squeezing Ben's fingers.

He squeezed back, but he couldn't get his throat to work.

Ernie clapped his hands. "Let's hit the road!"

"Ernie and Pastor Chris are driving the RVs," Marley said. "I'm taking Ernie's pickup. Would you mind riding with me?"

Finding his voice, Ben answered, "Sounds great. Be right there." He crossed the parking lot to where his uncle waited with his duffel bag.

"You have a good trip, son." Uncle Steve set the bag at their feet before giving Ben a back-thumping hug. "When you get cell-phone reception again on the trip home, give me a call and I'll be here to pick you up."

Once more, Ben's stomach tensed at the thought of his state-of-the-art smartphone becoming virtually useless for several days. If nothing else, he could snap photos with it. Definitely not of Marley's caliber, but at least he could document this excursion into unfamiliar territory.

Behind him, the RV engines rumbled. Ben scooped up his duffel bag, wiggled his fingers in a reluctant farewell to his uncle, then trotted over to where Marley waited in Ernie's blue pickup. A tarp covered the mound of supplies filling the back.

Marley watched with a smile as Ben shoved his bag into the space behind the seat. As soon as he climbed in and buckled his seat belt, she threw the gearshift into Drive and circled the lot until they were directly behind the two RVs. She reached for a two-way radio clipped to the visor and clicked the button. "Right behind you and ready to roll."

"Ten-four," was Ernie's scratchy reply.

"Heading out," Pastor Chris echoed.

Before long, they'd left the city of Alpine behind, and Ben settled in for the ride. Marley had stocked the cab with a thermos of coffee, bottled water, several packages of string cheese and a bag of trail mix. As soon as they hit open road, she asked Ben to refill her travel mug. She'd even thought to bring an extra mug for Ben. "Hope you don't need cream or sugar," she said. "Condiments are with the rest of the food in the RVs."

"Black's fine." Ben took a careful sip from his mug. "How long a drive are we in for?"

"About three hours. We should reach Candelaria in plenty of time for lunch. I bet the ladies already have the tamales ready to steam."

"Homemade tamales? Why didn't you say

so? I'd have been first in line to sign up for this trip."

Marley slanted him a crooked grin. "If I'd known that's all it took…"

He met her gaze, his voice softening. "Don't kid yourself. Even without the tamales, you're quite a persuasive woman, Ms. Sanders."

With a faltering breath, she tightened her grip on the steering wheel and glued her gaze to the highway. Forgetting about his own misgivings, Ben took quiet pleasure in observing how his words affected her. Behind a camera, teaching a photography class, or helping to organize a fund-raising event, Marley oozed confidence. But every once in a while—like when he'd picked her up at her office for the shopping trip—Ben glimpsed the vulnerability she hid so well.

With a subdued sigh, he shifted to stare out the window at the flat, barren terrain—not so different from the landscape of his heart when he'd arrived in Alpine back in September. But spending time at the ranch, getting to know Marley, helping with her outreach team… Marley had promised this trip to Candelaria would change him, but he couldn't deny that parts of him were already changing. Maybe not the faith part—but returning to big-city life and the corporate rat race didn't sound quite so appealing anymore.

Not to mention the type of jobs he was searching for were scarce. Maybe he should look more seriously at e-tail companies, or set his sights on smaller operations. Or, as Marley had suggested, consider teaching.

Yep, he was beginning to accept he might need to adjust his goals slightly. Or a lot, if he caved to pressure from his aunt and uncle and decided to make Alpine his permanent home.

He glanced over at Marley. Another superstrong reason to consider sticking around.

Spotting a cell tower on the horizon, Ben noticed they were nearing Marfa. Might be his best chance for decent cell coverage. Out of habit more than anything, he tugged his phone from his jeans pocket and tapped the mail icon.

The message list came up empty. He hissed out a sharp breath.

Marley looked over. "You okay?"

He was almost embarrassed to answer. "You know me, always checking for any response to my résumés."

"It's Saturday. They're probably all out yachting or playing golf or whatever executives do on weekends." Her tone suggested she couldn't think of a more frivolous waste of time.

"Don't knock it till you've tried it. Golf is

very relaxing." Ben missed the expensive set of golf clubs he'd left in his closet back at the condo. If he needed to, he could sell the clubs to pay another month's rent.

"It isn't the game I object to. It's what goes on—" Marley pursed her lips. "Never mind."

Now she'd made him curious. "Don't tell me. Your heart was broken by a rogue golfer."

She didn't reply right away, which made Ben wonder even more. "Let's just say I once knew a rich guy whose priorities were totally messed up. Golf wasn't the disease, but it became one of the more obvious symptoms."

This was a side of Marley Ben hadn't seen before. He watched her carefully as he asked, "Is he still in your life?"

"Not in any way that matters." She sighed. "And now it's definitely time to change the subject. How about some trail mix? My 5 a.m. bowl of cereal is wearing off."

What was it about Ben Fisher that threatened Marley's resolve about keeping all those secret places in her life locked firmly away? She had to keep reminding herself she'd barely met the guy three months ago.

But these stirrings in her heart kept reminding her she wanted things to be different. To be fully herself with someone who accepted everything about her, because she wouldn't be the person she was today if not for overcoming the mistakes of the past.

Why now, Lord? Why him?

This would be a lot easier if she didn't also sense his interest in her—which, obviously, he resisted with equal determination. He knew as well as she did that the timing was all wrong.

They were well past Marfa now, driving through the rugged terrain along US-67. Buttes, mesas and rocky ridges broke up the landscape of rolling hills. Up ahead, the angle of the morning sun on a rust-colored bluff caught Marley's eye. She snatched the two-way radio off the visor. "Hey, y'all. I'm pulling over to take some photos. Don't get too far ahead, okay?"

Pastor Chris's crackling voice responded. "Slowin' it down. Don't take too long, though. I can almost smell those tamales from here!"

Laughing, Marley promised she'd hurry. Easing the pickup onto the shoulder, she shifted into Park, then reached behind the seat for her camera. Pushing open the door, she grinned over her shoulder. "Come on, Ben. You can be my rattlesnake lookout."

As she stepped around to the front of the pickup, she noticed Ben hadn't budged. He'd also left his window rolled up tight. She marched over, yanked his door open and motioned him to get out. "I was only half-kidding."

"I figured." Ben folded his arms and faced forward in his seat. "That's why I'm staying put."

"Okay, just have the snakebite kit ready. I'm pretty sure Ernie keeps it in the glove compartment." Marley returned to the front of the pickup and framed a shot in her digital viewfinder. By the time she'd taken several photos, she was already envisioning the creative enhancements she planned to try back at the studio.

"Spectacular."

At the sound of Ben's voice behind her, Marley nearly jumped out of her skin. "I didn't hear you get out of the pickup."

"Since I couldn't find the snakebite kit, I decided I'd better keep an eye out after all."

"Nice of you to care." Marley hiked a brow and turned to snap more photos.

"Oooh, good one." Ben peered at the camera monitor, his breath warm against Marley's neck. "Who knew rocks could be so many different colors?"

She shifted to glare at him. "The rattlesnakes would be on the ground, you know."

"I figure they took one look at me and my killer sneakers, then hightailed it back to their den."

Shaking her head, Marley took one last shot before striding past Ben and climbing back into the pickup cab. As soon as he joined her, she got on the two-way radio to tell Pastor Chris they were on the road again.

"I was serious, you know," Ben said after several minutes.

She glanced his way with a smirk. "About what? Your killer sneakers?"

The look he returned was anything but joking. "I mean your photos. They're amazing. If you were in a city like Houston or Dallas—"

"I wouldn't be surrounded by scenery like this to photograph."

That silenced him for a moment. "Point taken. But you've got real talent, Marley. In the right market, you could be raking in big bucks."

"I like where I am just fine." After ten years in Alpine, she couldn't imagine living anywhere else. She also couldn't deny Ben's appreciation for her photography skills always touched a deep place in her heart, the place where she craved acknowledgment not only of her talent, but also who she was...who she *really* was.

They'd come to a section of roadway with several curves and sharp bends, and Marley had to pay close attention to her driving. Though her neck and shoulders would soon be in knots, at least she had an excuse to call a halt to this line of conversation.

After Pastor Chris and Ernie radioed to check on her a couple of times, Ben must have heard the tension in her tone. "Want me to drive awhile?"

"I'm okay. We're almost to the final stretch." She cast him a lopsided smile. "Anyway, this is your first trip to Candelaria. I want you to be able to appreciate the scenery. When we turn up ahead, you'll get a taste of what those kids have to endure on their bus ride to and from school in Presidio every day."

Ben nodded without replying. Twenty minutes later, she slowed behind the two RVs as the road they traveled ended at FM 170. "Mexico is straight ahead," Marley explained. "We're just a few miles from the Rio Grande." She nodded to her right. "In forty-eight miles we'll be in Candelaria."

Ben glanced left. "And that direction is Presidio?"

"In another mile or so."

"Where the schools are."

"Right."

From the set of his mouth, Marley guessed

Ben was finally beginning to appreciate exactly how isolated Candelaria was.

"Marley! Welcome back, *mija*!" Conchita Montero nearly smothered Marley as she enfolded her in plump brown arms.

"I missed you, too, Conchita." Giving the woman a final squeeze, Marley stepped back. "How have you been? Is your knee any better?"

"It is no worse, which is a good thing, no?" Conchita hooked her arm around Marley's waist as they watched the college students unload the pickup into a nearby storage shed.

"Be sure you tell the doctor about it next time he's here." Marley glanced around at the mothers and children who'd come out to greet the team. "Where's your daughter? I'm dying to meet your new grandson."

Conchita's round face beamed with pride. "Rosalinda is in *la casa*. It's feeding time for our *niño*. Miguelito is a healthy, growing boy!" She nudged Marley toward the shade of a blue tarp, where a few of the women tended steaming pans and kettles over outdoor grills. "Lunch is ready. We will eat as soon as your people finish."

"Smells wonderful!" Marley rested a hand on her growling stomach. "I've been telling our new volunteers how good your tamales are."

Conchita lifted a pot lid, stirred some beans and sampled a taste. She nodded her satisfaction. "This one is not so spicy." She winked. "For you *gringos*."

Just then, Ben ambled over. "Don't hold back the jalapeños on my account."

Marley laughed. "Conchita Montero, meet Ben Fisher. Ben is Steve and Jane Whitlow's nephew from Houston, and I hear he likes his Mexican food extra-spicy."

"My pleasure, Mrs. Montero." Ben pushed back his ball cap. "You must be Lucas's mother. We were glad to have his help with the trail ride last month."

The woman beamed. "So he has told me. You will see him again at the end of your visit."

"So Rosalinda Cortez is your daughter, right? My aunt sent something for the new baby."

Marley smiled to herself. She'd been concerned about Ben's awkwardness around people so far removed from his sphere of experience, but if he felt any discomfort, he showed no outward signs. On the other hand, as a businessman with strong PR skills, Ben seemed able to converse with anyone.

Unless the subject had to do with faith. Marley's prayers over this mission trip had included more than a few on Ben's behalf.

Noticing Chris, Ernie and the Tech students

striding over from the storage shed, Marley turned to Conchita. "Looks like the hungry hordes are ready for lunch."

"Save me a seat," Ben said with a quick tug on Marley's ponytail. "I'll run and get the gift for Rosalinda."

Conchita chuckled softly, winking as she handed Marley a plate and utensils. "Your new boyfriend is very handsome."

"Oh, no, we're just friends." With a self-conscious smile, Marley held out her plate while a young woman served her huge helpings of rice, beans and tamales.

"Don't fool yourself. He has eyes only for you, *mija*."

Marley refused to acknowledge the flutter in her chest. She grabbed a cup of iced tea and found a place at the end of a long wooden picnic table. If she couldn't get her growing feelings for Ben under control, the visit to Candelaria she'd so looked forward to might turn out to be the longest four days of her life.

With the gift from Aunt Jane tucked under his arm, Ben jogged back to the food tent. He glanced around for Mrs. Montero, but when he didn't find her right away, he accepted a plate of food. The day was mild and sunny with a slight breeze, perfect for dining al fresco. Ben scanned the picnic area looking for Marley. When he saw she was surrounded by several of the local women and children, he plopped down in the only empty spot, next to Ernie Coutu.

Ernie spooned rice and beans into a corn tortilla and folded it burrito-style. "Best part of coming down here is the food. Hot and spicy, just the way I like it."

"Sure smells good." Ben peeled the corn husk off a tamale and sliced off a bite with the edge of his fork. When he sampled the savory shredded pork wrapped in cornmeal, his taste buds shimmied with delight. "Wow."

"What'd I tell you? Better than the best Tex-Mex restaurants Alpine has to offer."

Better than anything Ben had tasted in Houston, as well. He finished off his meal and went back for seconds. He would have taken thirds but decided not to be greedy. Anyway, he wasn't about to get in the way of the Texas Tech boys. A couple of them were built like linebackers, and they didn't look willing to share.

After helping to clear tables, Ben spotted Marley as she started across the road with Mrs. Montero. He called her name and hurried to catch up, squinting against the bright afternoon glare. "I've still got this package from Aunt Jane and didn't want Mrs. Montero to get away."

"Ah, *bueno.*" The older woman gestured toward the small frame house in front of them. "Rosalinda is inside. We are coming to see the baby. You will come, too?"

"Uh, sure." Ben followed the ladies up the cracked concrete steps and into a neatly furnished living room.

A young mother sat rocking her baby and crooning a lilting Spanish lullaby. She beamed a smile as they entered. "Hi, Marley. Come meet Miguel."

"He's adorable!" Marley stepped closer and ruffled the baby's thick, dark curls. "Rosalinda, this is my friend Ben. He brought something for you."

Ben held out the gift. "It's from my aunt."

"*Gracias.*" Eyes wide, Rosalinda shifted her infant son into the crook of her arm so that both hands were free. She slid a thumbnail beneath the edge of the wrapping paper and carefully tore open the gift.

Ben immediately recognized the pale yellow baby blanket his aunt had been knitting when he'd first arrived in Alpine. Back then, he'd never expected to actually meet the young mother for whom the gift was intended.

"It's beautiful, and so soft!" Marley fingered the scalloped edge. "Almost makes me wish I'd learned to knit."

One hand on her daughter's shoulder, Mrs.

Montero glanced between Marley and Ben. A knowing smile creased her plump cheeks. "I think perhaps you are wishing for a family of your own."

With a nervous laugh, Marley locked her arms across her chest and edged away from Rosalinda. "Someday, maybe."

Feeling none too comfortable himself, Ben rolled the brim of his ball cap and angled one foot toward the door. "I should go see what everybody else is up to. Nice meeting you, ladies."

"Tell Ernie and Pastor Chris I'll be right there," Marley said.

With a quick nod, Ben tugged his cap low over his eyes and escaped. Without thinking, he tugged out his cell phone to check for messages and email, but the No Service message mocked him. His stomach curdled with the sudden overwhelming sense of being utterly disconnected—not just from cell service, but from everything that mattered.

Chapter Ten

By Saturday evening, the outreach team had a good start on some of the odd jobs they'd planned to take care of for the Candelaria families. Pastor Chris had organized the team into four groups, placing Ben with the two linebacker types. Fortunately, they had a lot more handyman experience than he did, and the three of them had spent most of Saturday afternoon tearing down and completely rebuilding the dilapidated picket fence around Mrs. Montero's vegetable garden.

In many ways, the work was even more labor-intensive than what Uncle Steve had Ben doing around the ranch. Ben's muscles screamed from the effort, but he found unexpected satisfaction in wielding a posthole digger and swinging a hammer. He might even call the labor therapeutic, because it certainly left him little energy to ponder the confusing path his life had taken these past several weeks.

On Sunday morning, Pastor Chris led a worship service in the town's little Catholic church. Ben hadn't planned to attend, but Marley cornered him as he sipped coffee under a mesquite tree. She didn't exactly drag him into the church, but the determined set of her mouth told him it would be easier to yield than to offer up excuses. He followed her through the heavy wooden doors of the white stucco building but resolutely resisted her nudge toward a front pew, choosing instead to sit near the doors so he could slip out quickly if the urge struck him.

He did duck out before the closing song, but he hadn't missed a word of Pastor Chris's message. The whole thing about not hiding your light under a bushel, being light and salt to the world, just like they were doing here in Candelaria. And then something from Jeremiah about God knowing His plans for His children.

That afternoon, as he pounded the last nail in a fence slat, he glanced up to see Mrs. Montero watching from her back porch. She waved him over.

"Yes, ma'am?" Ben wiped his grubby hands on his jeans as he walked over.

"This is the Lord's day. Your work will wait."

The plump woman pointed to Ben's arms. "And see? The sun is burning you."

Mrs. Montero was right—the skin below his rolled-up sleeves was beginning to look more red than tan. He hadn't given any thought to using sunscreen in December, apparently a mistake. He turned to the college boys still hard at work on the fence. "Let's take a break and cool off in the RV for a couple of hours."

The young men didn't argue. Laying down their tools, they slogged across the road to where the RVs were parked, the windows cranked open to let the mild desert breezes flow through.

"Come into my kitchen and sit awhile." Mrs. Montero held open her screen door.

Weighing the choice between Mrs. Montero's company and an RV full of big, sweaty college jocks, Ben didn't take long to make up his mind. He followed her inside, where she offered him a seat in a red vinyl dinette chair. One elbow propped on the table, he stretched out his legs while she brought two chilled sodas from the refrigerator.

Neither spoke for a few minutes, and Ben felt the awkwardness as he silently sipped his drink. Mrs. Montero seemed to be sizing him up, so he sat a little straighter and offered a hesitant smile. She nodded thoughtfully.

Ben cleared his throat. "I hope I'm not keeping you from anything."

"Not at all. You make me very curious, however."

"Me?"

"*Sí.* Many have come to Candelaria bringing help or things we need. You are…different."

Avoiding her gaze, Ben set down his soft drink can and slowly twirled it on the tabletop. "I'm here to help just like everybody else."

"You are a hard worker, it is true. But sometimes people come who are…" The woman massaged her forehead. "I think you would say *cynic.*"

Stung, Ben pursed his lips. "You doubt my motives for being here?"

"No, I think you are a good person. But I watched you in church this morning. Something troubles you. I think you are here not so much to help my town but to find yourself." Mrs. Montero's gaze softened, and she laid her callused brown hand upon Ben's arm. "Maybe you will also find God."

While the men handled some of the odd jobs the Candelaria families needed help with, Marley and the women from Texas Tech gathered several of the children together inside the church to make Christmas crafts and share a devotional.

"Miss Marley, come and see." Eleven-year-old Isabella sat on the chancel step, where she worked on a watercolor painting of the Nativity.

Isabella, the same little girl from the school bus photo, held a special place in Marley's heart. Marley kneeled and tugged on the girl's long, thick braid. "Wow, that's the most beautiful Christmas star I've ever seen!"

Isabella swirled her paintbrush in a cup of water. "I'm going to give this to Tío Lucas when he comes for the fiesta."

Another child called Marley over to look at her drawing, and soon it was time to send the kids home. Marley and her helpers gathered up Bibles and art supplies, then headed over to the RV to make supper for the team.

As they finished cleaning up, Marley noticed the sun was at a perfect angle for sunset photography, so she stepped inside the women's RV to retrieve her camera. She wandered down the road to where the pavement ended and found Ben seated on a rock and staring toward the western sky. Something about his pensive profile brought a catch to her throat. She lifted her camera and snapped a photo.

He must have heard the shutter. Glancing over his shoulder, he offered a crooked smile. "Collecting blackmail material?"

"Maybe. Workaholic caught enjoying the sunset—should be worth a grand or two." Marley strolled up beside him, her gaze following his. "This is my favorite time of day. Did you ever see such amazing colors?"

"It is pretty amazing." Ben scooted over to make room for her on his rock. When she sat down next to him, he added, "You're pretty amazing, too."

Warmth flooded her cheeks, in direct opposition to the coolness of the rock seeping through her jeans. She fiddled with a camera setting. "I'm just doing what I love."

"It shows. You really know how to relate to these people. It's equally obvious how much they care about you."

"If they do, it's only because I care about *them*."

Ben grew silent, hands braced on his knees. He exhaled long and slow. "This afternoon Mrs. Montero called me a cynic."

"Oh, Ben." Sensing his turmoil, Marley almost reached for his hand but thought better of it and covered by brushing a strand of hair off her face. "I'm sure she didn't mean to be hurtful."

"No, but she made her point all the same."

Hoping to lighten the mood, she gave him a friendly poke in the ribs. "So…you admit she has a point?"

He shot her a sidelong glance. "I've spent the last three months—more like the past couple of years, if I'm completely honest—being told by everyone I care about that I need an attitude adjustment. I'm not saying I disagree, but to be nailed by a perfect stranger? That was a bit disconcerting."

Weighing her reply, Marley remembered a photo she'd taken a few weeks ago during her photography class. She set the camera on view mode and scrolled backward until she found the photo she searched for. She held it up for Ben to see. "Recognize this guy?"

He studied the picture, then chuckled. "That was a fun day."

"Yep, not a cynical line on your face." Marley smiled at the image of Ben posing for the kids. He'd struck a bodybuilder stance, looking tough and macho except for the clownish grin. "I like you best when you're just being yourself, not—"

She bit the inside of her lip before she said more than she should.

Twisting to face her, Ben narrowed his gaze. "Finish what you were saying. I can take it."

"I don't have any right to criticize your life or your career ambitions." Marley rose and strode a few steps away, pretending to focus in on a camera shot.

"But you clearly want to. You've been judging me ever since I first walked into your studio." Hands thrust into his jacket pockets, Ben stood beside her. "I've never represented myself as anything other than who I am. If you can't accept me, it's your problem, not mine."

His words stabbed deep, not so much at the realization of how she'd judged him, but because of the lie she herself was living. Would he still accept her if her past ever came to light?

The sinking sun crowned a distant ridge with an apricot glow, and Marley lifted her camera before she let the picture slip away. Seven shots later, she released a tired sigh and shut off the camera. "You're right, I had some preconceived opinions about you. But then you came up with the trail-ride idea. You bent over backward to get our event publicized and make it a success. You followed me through nearly every store in town shopping for Christmas gifts. And now you're here, pitching in like you've always been a part of the team. You've been…amazing."

"Amazing?" Ben edged in front of Marley and ran his finger beneath the limp strands of hair that kept falling across her eyes. "Seems like a few minutes ago I used the same word to describe you."

She shivered inwardly at his touch and took one giant step backward. "It'll be dark soon. We'd better go back."

"Marley." Ben's hand clamped down on her wrist, and she had no choice but to halt and look at him. But in the fading light his expression was unreadable. A full second passed before his fingers relaxed and he released her arm. "Yeah, you're right. We'd better go back."

Ben watched Marley walk away, and the ache in his belly became a gaping pit. Coming to Candelaria had been a mistake—a huge one. Bad enough the perceptive Mrs. Montero had pegged him so easily.

Worse, he couldn't escape his growing feelings for Marley no matter how hard he tried to deny them.

He couldn't say for sure when he first became aware of how much her opinion of him mattered. It might have been the day he'd run into her outside the department store and enlisted her help in picking out some less citified clothes. Or possibly when he saw the delight in her eyes after he suggested the trail ride.

Face it, Marley makes you want to be a better person than you know you are.

Raucous laughter met him as he approached the men's RV. Probably a continuation of the sports trivia game the guys had started Saturday night. Not up to racking his brain for who won the 1963 Heisman Trophy or which teams competed in the 1994 Super Bowl, Ben declined Pastor Chris's invitation to join the game and sidled down the narrow passageway to the bathroom. After scrubbing away the day's sweat and grime, he climbed into his bunk.

Tired as he was, sleep didn't come easy, and not just because of the noise from the other end of the RV. Sounds of hammers, saws and swishing paintbrushes echoed through his thoughts, along with images of Marley surrounded by laughing, dark-haired school children on their way into the little white church. Marley had found a calling, a cause that stretched and inspired her, and here he was still wobbling on the broken rungs of his career ladder.

He had an MBA, for crying out loud. It ought to be worth something besides occupying the top shelf of his bedroom closet back in Houston. Some days it felt as if he'd left his self-respect behind along with his diploma.

Maybe if he could come up with a long-term strategy to help this town Marley cared so much about, he could earn back a little of her admiration…and perhaps rebuild the confidence he'd lost along with his job. He fell asleep sometime after midnight with those thoughts running through his mind.

The next morning, when the aromas of sizzling sausage, peppers, tomatoes and onions roused him, an idea started percolating right along with the morning coffee. After he'd shaved in the tiny bathroom and donned a fresh set of work clothes for the day, Ben ambled into the kitchenette. Most of the men were already up and wolfing down breakfast. Ernie stood over a skillet of scrambled eggs and spooned them into the flour tortillas Pastor Chris held out for him.

"Just in time for breakfast burritos." Chris handed Ben a plate. "These tortillas are fresh as they come. Mrs. Montero brought them over a few minutes ago."

"Thanks. Smells great!" Ben grabbed a cup of coffee and wedged himself into the booth next to his two linebacker buddies.

Seconds later, the RV door flew open and five disgruntled women barged in, Marley in the lead. "Hey, you! Not fair! When were you planning on telling us breakfast was ready?"

"Uh, never." Ernie spread his arms wide to keep Marley from grabbing the plate he'd just filled. "This is a man's breakfast. Go back to your own trailer and eat your yogurt and granola."

If not for their teasing grins, Ben might be worried they'd come to blows. Finally Ernie relented and handed Marley the plate, but not without an exaggerated show of annoyance. She passed it to one of the Tech girls, who carried it outside, where there was more room, and then waited for the next serving to be ready.

By the time the four college women had been served and Marley accepted a plate for herself, Ben had finished his breakfast. He refilled his coffee cup and followed Marley outside. When she settled into one of the folding camp chairs, Ben found an empty one and moved it next to hers.

Marley glanced his way with a tentative smile. "Too crowded in there for you?"

"Actually, I hoped we could talk." Ben hesitated to bring up his ideas in front of the students. If Marley shot him down, he doubted what was left of his pride could handle the public humiliation.

Dropping her voice to a whisper, Marley began, "If this is about last night..."

"No. I mean, sort of." Ben paused as two of the women finished eating and excused themselves. The other two sat far enough away that they couldn't easily overhear. "My corporate background was an asset for publicizing the trail ride, right?"

Marley had just bitten into her burrito and had to chew and swallow before she replied. "Yes, of course it was. What are you getting at, Ben?"

Jaw clenched, he stared into his coffee cup. "What I'm trying to say is, as much as I can see the value in what your team is doing here, there's got to be something more we can do, something that could give these people a real shot at a better life."

Marley took another bite and then laid her burrito on her plate. Shifting sideways, she tilted her head. "You've worked on one fund-raiser and spent two whole days here. Do you honestly think you can come up with answers nobody else has thought of?"

Ben inhaled a shallow breath. "But I have an idea. Do you want to hear it or not?"

"I'm listening."

By now, the other two college women had returned to their RV, leaving Ben and Marley alone under the awning. Ben hoped the guys would stay inside awhile longer and give them some privacy. "It occurred to me that as good as the women in this town cook—the tamales we had Saturday, these melt-in-your-mouth tortillas—they could start their own catering business."

Marley's jaw dropped. "Catering? Are you serious? How many times do I have to tell you the nearest town of any size is fifty miles away?"

"Yeah, I get it. We'd have some logistics to work out—"

"Ben. Get real." Marley shoved up from her chair. "You're talking cold storage, transportation, advertising—what you're suggesting is a whole lot more complicated than selling arts and crafts on consignment."

"Yes, but it's not impossible." Ben set his cup on the ground, then rose and spread his hands. "With all the churches and other groups already supporting outreach to the town, I bet you wouldn't have any problem getting donations and volunteers."

"Even if we could—and that's a big *if*—don't forget, there's no internet or cell service here. Not to mention there must be all kinds of legal hurdles related to obtaining a food license." With a quick glance around, Marley lowered her voice. "I told you, Ben, it's very likely several of the townspeople aren't even US citizens. You start involving government regulations and you could cause real problems."

"I'm sorry. I didn't think—"

"No, you didn't." Marley squeezed her eyes shut, shoulders heaving. When she looked at Ben again, her expression had softened. "The interest you've taken in Candelaria means the world to me, even more that you cared enough to spend time coming up with the catering idea. It's just not feasible under the circumstances."

Ben gave a reluctant nod. Seemed he couldn't get things right even when he consciously tried.

The screen door on the RV creaked open and Ernie tromped down the steps, followed by the two college men he'd been working with. "We're heading over to finish painting the Gonzales house. Y'all got your marching orders for the day?"

"The girls are sprucing up the playground this morning," Marley said. She crossed to the door and handed her dishes up to Pastor Chris. "Then we're doing more Christmas crafts this afternoon, plus some cleanup and setup for the fiesta tomorrow."

"Good." Ernie opened a storage compartment under the RV. He hauled out a toolbox, painting supplies, pruning shears and a hoe, then passed the gardening tools to Marley. "Ben, you and your guys can help Chris's team finish up the shed roof."

"Sure thing." As Ben's muscle-bound cohorts exited the RV, he steeled himself for another day of hard labor under the high-desert sun. But as he hefted the toolbox, Pastor Chris leaned out the door.

"Don't take off yet, Ben." Chris handed down a set of keys and a yellow sheet of paper torn from a legal pad. "You're the designated gofer today. I need you to take Ernie's pickup to Presidio and pick up the supplies on this list. Directions to the hardware store are on the back."

Surprised and a little bit insulted, Ben scowled. Guess he knew his value to the team. He scanned the paper. Shingles, roofing nails, toilet seal, faucet washers. "Do I charge it or what?"

"The church has an account," Chris said. "All you have to do is sign for it."

"Better fill the gas tank, too." Ernie handed Ben a wad of cash. "And why don't you pick up six or eight frozen pizzas for tonight's supper. There's a supermarket a few blocks from the hardware store."

Ben stuffed the money into his jeans pocket and tried to keep his tone civil. "Anything else?"

Ernie shot Chris a questioning glance. At Chris's shrug, Ernie tipped his head toward Ben and narrowed one eye. "Just take good care of my baby. She doesn't handle quite like your 'Stang."

"Gotcha." Ben tried to look on the bright side as he marched to the pickup. He'd be sitting in a comfortable vehicle most of the morning instead of increasing his calluses on a shed roof. And Presidio might be big enough to have decent cell-phone service so he could check messages and email. He still held out hope that some of those résumés he'd sent out had generated some interview requests.

Sure would be nice to feel competent at something again.

Chapter Eleven

Sipping a tall glass of iced tea, Marley stood in the shade of the RV awning and stared up the long, empty stretch of highway. It shimmered like a mirage under the noonday sun. Ben should have been back from Presidio by now. What was taking so long?

She glanced over at Pastor Chris as he polished off a ham sandwich. "You could have sent one of the students, you know."

Chris dabbed his lips and then wadded up his napkin. "I figured he'd appreciate the break."

"This is a new experience for Ben. He's trying hard."

"Yeah, I can see that." Rising, Chris came to stand next to Marley. "I'm not sure he's doing any of this for the right reasons, though. It's like he's trying to prove something. Not necessarily to us, but to himself."

Marley couldn't argue. Thinking back to her earlier conversation with Ben, she laughed softly. "Do you know what he suggested to me this morning? A catering business, here in Candelaria."

"Catering? An interesting proposition, but…" Chris gave his head a disbelieving shake. "I hope you explained why it wouldn't work."

"I tried." Even so, she couldn't help being touched by how much thought Ben had put into the idea. Beneath his big-city attitude and—yes—a recurring case of cynicism, the guy had a good heart.

Over by the old school building, several children romped on the playground, their laughter burbling on the mild breeze. Remarkable how kids could entertain themselves for hours with nothing more high-tech than a swing set or a basketball. Marley couldn't help wondering how different her life might have been if she'd grown up learning to appreciate the simpler things of life.

Instead, she'd learned Daddy's money could buy her anything. Or buy her out of whatever trouble she got herself into. The first time anyone ever told her she *couldn't* have her own way was when Valerie Bishop, who later married Healy Ferguson, confronted her for shoplifting, and then testified against her in juvenile court.

Accepting responsibility for her own actions was a hard lesson for the old Marsha Sanderson, and not one she learned right away. Thank God for Healy and Valerie, or Marley might never have found her way after her reckless driving almost cost Tina's life.

Pastor Chris interrupted her thoughts with a noisy sigh. "Guess it's about time to get back to work."

"Yeah, I need to head over to the church." Draining her iced tea glass, Marley crunched an ice chip. She started to duck into the RV to dispose of her glass, but as the pastor held the door for her, she stopped midstride and peered at him thoughtfully. "Do you think anyone ever does anything good for purely unselfish reasons?"

His brow wrinkled. "I suppose not. But even when we have our own agenda, it doesn't affect God's ability to bless our efforts." A knowing smile stole across his lips. "Ben's included."

Hers, too, Marley hoped. Perhaps someday she'd confide in the pastor about her need to atone for her messed-up past.

After a quick cleanup of the lunch dishes, Marley strolled toward the glistening white church building. When she heard the rumble of tires on pavement, her heart rolled over in her chest and a relieved sigh rippled through her.

Hoisting a couple of sacks and an insulated

shopping bag, Ben climbed from the pickup. Marley waved and met him near the back of the RV. "I was getting worried. Everything go okay in town?"

"Only got lost twice." He grinned. "Better get these pizzas in the freezer. Then I want to show you something."

"If it has anything to do with toilet parts, I'll pass." Seeing the Tech girls directing several kids into the church building, Marley called to them that she'd be over in a few minutes. She followed Ben into the RV and leaned against the counter as he jammed pizzas into the tiny freezer. At least he seemed in a much better mood than when she'd shot down his catering idea. Maybe the drive to town actually helped.

"Come sit down." Ben motioned Marley to the table. She scooted into the booth and Ben slid in beside her. He laid a folded newspaper in front of her.

"What's this?"

"While I was at the supermarket, I saw they had some big-city newspapers on the rack. Thought I'd see what's been happening in the world the last couple of days, so I bought this El Paso paper." Ben flipped to page six and grinned. "Look what I found staring me in the face."

The headline over a half-page article read

Riders for Candelaria: Alpine Community Digs Deep to Support Struggling Border Town. Neil Ingram's byline appeared below, along with several photos she hadn't seen published before from the trail ride.

A tingle of curiosity mixed with apprehension started deep in Marley's abdomen. "El Paso? I didn't realize we did any publicity that far away."

"We didn't. The wire services must have picked up the story. And look, they credited you on a couple of the photos they ran. That ought to bring you more business."

Despite her misgivings, she couldn't help imagining how this kind of positive publicity could help keep her in her studio.

Then she glimpsed the photo in the lower left-hand corner. It featured her along with Pastor Chris and Ernie, and identified them as "the backbone of Spirit Outreach." She'd tactfully asked Neil not to print this photo, but he must have forgotten when supplying the El Paso paper with images to go with the article. Marley could only imagine her father's reaction if someone from her past happened upon the photo and recognized her as Marsha Sanderson.

"Marley?" Ben cocked his head, brows slanted in a concerned look.

"I, uh, wasn't expecting this. It's a little scary."

"But it's good, right? Good for Candelaria *and* for you."

"I don't know. Maybe." She gripped the edge of the table and slid sideways, forcing Ben to let her out of the booth. "The kids are waiting. I need to get over to the church."

Stunned by Marley's baffling response to the newspaper piece, Ben almost chased her across the hard-packed ground to make her explain. He shook his head in confusion.

Someone called his name. He glanced left to see Ernie headed his way, no doubt in a hurry to get his hands on the supplies from town. With a groan, Ben trudged back inside the RV and gathered up the hardware-store bags. He met Ernie under the awning. "Got everything on the list. The shingles are in the back of the pickup." He fished a handful of bills and coins from his pocket. "Here's your change for the gas and pizzas."

"Thanks, Ben." Pocketing the money, Ernie peered into each bag, then gave a satisfied nod. "You want to run the roofing stuff over to Chris and the guys working on the shed? They could probably use a hand." He chuckled. "Unless you'd rather help fix a toilet."

His mind still on Marley, Ben doubted "How about neither?" would be an acceptable answer. "I'm probably safer with a hammer than a wrench."

"Suit yourself." Taking the plumbing supplies, Ernie jogged across the road.

Returning to the pickup, Ben drove over to the house where Pastor Chris and his team worked on the livestock shed, and for the rest of the afternoon he learned all about beams and joists, tar paper and shingles. A young mother with a toddler on her hip watched from a creaking glider on the back porch, then later greeted two older children as they bounded over from the church.

When the family disappeared inside the house, Ben felt a wave of sympathy for them. It had to be hard raising a family without their dad around. Marley had explained most of the husbands and fathers worked elsewhere, many on ranches on the Mexican side of the Rio Grande, and coming home for a visit could be difficult. With so few men in town, it was no wonder the women were grateful for help with the more labor-intensive chores.

As Ben passed another shingle to Pastor Chris, he thought about his own father. True, things had gotten tense between them after Mom died and Paula entered the picture, but at least Dad had always been around when Ben and Aidan were growing up.

Right now, Ben couldn't help wishing his dad had done a better job of teaching him some handyman skills. Maybe when Ben got back to Houston, he'd offer to help with the kitchen re-model his father and Paula had been planning. It couldn't hurt to extend the olive branch and let his dad know he was at least trying to move toward acceptance.

He laughed to himself. Was this part of the attitude adjustment Aunt Jane had been praying for?

"Ben. Ben!" Pastor Chris's voice sliced through his thoughts, startling him. "Slide the box of roofing nails closer, will you?"

"Sorry. My mind was wandering."

"No kidding." Chris's hammer rang out as he secured another shingle into place. Sitting back on his heels, he tugged off stained leather work gloves. "That should do it. I'm ready to call it a day."

Ben was more than ready. Sitting atop a black roof under the afternoon glare of the high-desert sun? Cheapest sauna ever. He wasted no time following Chris down the ladder, then helped gather up tools and leftover shingles. They tossed everything into the pickup bed, and with Chris and the Tech students riding on the tailgate, Ben drove the pickup back to the RV.

Inside, Chris went to the fridge and tossed

everyone an ice-cold sports drink. The Tech boys carried their drinks outside under the awning, and Chris slid into the booth across from Ben. He released a tired chuckle. "It could be worse. Try doing this in the middle of summer."

"It's definitely the hardest work I've done in a long, long time." Ben wrapped his hands around the drink bottle and let the coolness seep into his blistered palms.

"I hope you're not sorry you came."

Ben scraped his teeth across his lower lip. "It's been an eye-opener, that's for sure. But no, I'm not sorry. Every day I understand a little better how much this town means to Marley."

"Don't be mad, but…she told me about the idea you suggested."

"The catering thing? Yeah, I see now how impractical it would be. I just hoped—" Ben massaged the bridge of his nose.

Pastor Chris folded his arms along the edge of the table. "We all wish we could do more, but the situation is what it is, so we do the best we can."

Someone had moved the El Paso newspaper to the end of the table. Ben reached for it and opened it to the trail-ride article. "Look what I found in town this morning."

Chris's smile widened as his gaze skimmed

the page. "This is terrific, exactly the kind of coverage we need to bring more attention to what we're doing here."

"Then maybe you can explain something to me." Brow puckered, Ben described Marley's reaction to seeing the article. "I expected her to be as excited about it as you are, but then she just took off like it scared her."

Staring out the window, Pastor Chris sat in silence for a few moments. "There's a lot I don't understand about Marley. I had to accept a long time ago that she'll tell me when she's ready."

"You make her sound so mysterious."

"Isn't every woman a bit of a mystery?" A twisted smile crept across the pastor's lips. Then his eyes narrowed and he cocked his head. "You're getting serious about Marley, aren't you?"

The truth Ben could barely admit to himself drilled a hole in his gut. He fixed his gaze on the lime-green liquid swirling at the bottom of the plastic bottle. "I've never met anyone like her."

"But...?"

"But...as soon as I find a new job, I'll be leaving Alpine. It isn't fair to either one of us to let this grow into something more." Why did it suddenly hurt so much to speak those words aloud?

Using his thumbnail, Pastor Chris peeled away a torn corner of his drink label. "Who's to say you won't find work here? Maybe God brought you to Alpine for a reason."

Ben stiffened. "There are two things you should know about me, Pastor, if you haven't figured them out already. Number one, as Marley is so fond of reminding me, I'm a city boy through and through. And number two…" He clenched his jaw and looked the pastor directly in the eye. "I've been mad at God for a while now, so I seriously doubt He cares about me one way or the other."

Pastor Chris laced his fingers together and sat forward. "I can name more than a few city boys who adapted just fine to small-town living. In fact, the ones I know have never been happier."

Ben had to look away.

"As for God not caring about you," the pastor went on, "you couldn't be more wrong. Nothing—and I mean *nothing*—happens outside the Father's knowledge or control. So when it seems like everything is going wrong, at least according to *your* agenda, it probably just means God has a different agenda. This is when a wise man quits resisting and starts trusting."

It sounded so easy. *Too* easy. "What am I supposed to do—stop even trying to find another job because God's going to simply drop one into my lap?"

"You never know." The pastor's lazy grin rankled. At the sound of voices outside the RV, he slid from the booth. "Guess it's about time to stick those pizzas in the oven."

Ben sat chewing the inside of his lip while he watched Pastor Chris take the pizzas from the freezer and begin slitting open the plastic wrap. Once upon a time Ben had believed God had a plan for his life. And then, just when everything seemed to be going his way—*bam!* Instead of hope and a future, Ben's life started looking more like Job's.

He shifted to look out the window, his gaze sweeping the dusty little town and the mismatched array of cinderblock houses, trailers and sheds. And he had the audacity to compare his life to Job's? Shame filled him and he muttered a silent curse.

The RV door swung open and Ernie stepped inside. Ben glanced up to see Marley right behind him. Her lips quivered in a nervous smile before she sidled over to the kitchenette and asked Pastor Chris if he needed any help.

Ben took the opportunity to excuse himself. He needed time alone to think, because the cleanup and repair work they were doing on this mission trip didn't seem to stop at houses and playgrounds. He couldn't shake an unnerving sense that God was dragging him into His plan whether he liked it or not.

Chapter Twelve

Was it Tuesday already? Marley could hardly believe their brief time in Candelaria was almost at an end. Though she was bone-tired, nothing else in her life gave her such deep-down satisfaction. Even more beautiful was observing the changes in every group of volunteers the Spirit Outreach committee brought here, and these students from Texas Tech were no exception. The women had worked as hard as the men, painting and sprucing up in the mornings, then gathering the children for devotions and Christmas crafts in the afternoons. Marley had a feeling the Tech women had made lifelong friends with the children they'd mentored during this trip.

She observed equally touching responses in the men and would never forget how the biggest and brawniest Texas Tech guy turned blubbery when a stooped, gray-haired grandmother wrapped her arms around his neck to thank him for patching and painting her weathered front door.

Marley only wished she had a better sense of what was happening inside Ben's head and heart. He'd worked as hard as any of them, but since yesterday he'd grown disturbingly distant. Had she hurt his feelings so badly about the catering idea? Or was it her negative response to seeing her picture plastered across the page of a major Texas newspaper?

Probably both. In fact, looking back over the past few weeks, Marley figured she'd given off enough mixed signals to permanently shut down any interest Ben might have had in deepening their relationship.

She shouldn't care so much. When January rolled around, Ben would probably find himself overrun with job offers. Then he'd skedaddle faster than a scared horned toad.

So why, every time he glanced her way, did her heart do a hopeful little dance in her chest?

"Marley?" Pastor Chris's sneakers edged into her line of vision.

Straightening, she dropped a roll of masking tape into the supply crate she'd been packing. "What's up?"

"I was about to ask you the same thing. You looked like you were a million miles away."

"Just thinking about…everything." Her lips eased into a smile. "It's been another good trip."

"That it has." The pastor picked up a folded drop cloth and laid it in the crate.

Marley looked across the road, where Ben and two of the college guys applied the finishing touches on the house trim they'd been painting. Dribbles of dark green paint covered Ben's T-shirt, jeans and ball cap. A long sigh escaped from Marley's lips. Ben couldn't look more endearing if he tried.

Pastor Chris chuckled softly. "Admit it. You're smitten."

Her chin jerked backward. "What? No! I—I was just thinking I'll need another crate for the guys' supplies when they finish."

"You should give Ben a chance. He's a good man." The pastor shook his head. "Can't figure out why you two insist on fighting your feelings so hard."

Marley's stomach pinched. "Have you been talking to Ben about me?"

"Only enough to conclude there's something between you worth exploring." Brows slanted with concern, Pastor Chris glanced across the road, then back at Marley. "How long have you been in Alpine now—ten years? In all that time I've never known you to let a guy get close."

Arms crossed over her abdomen, Marley snorted a laugh. "How could I, when you and all my other friends at Spirit Fellowship insist on giving your seal of approval to anyone I show even the remotest interest in?"

"So sue us for looking out for you till the right guy comes along." The pastor's wink belied his serious tone.

"And you think the 'right guy' is Ben Fisher?"

"Can't say for sure, but I have a strong sense that God's at work here, and I wouldn't be surprised if His plan directly involves you and Ben."

His words sent a shiver down Marley's spine. "You know Ben doesn't intend to stay in Alpine. And I don't intend to leave."

"Even if God has other ideas?" When Marley had no argument, he went on, "I don't pretend to know what God has in mind. But I do know this—it's time to stop keeping people at arm's length. Eventually you have to let someone in."

Before Marley could respond, the pastor touched two fingers to his forehead in a mock salute and jogged across the road. His words lingered long after she finished packing up supplies and went inside the women's RV to freshen up.

That evening, the Candelarians had arranged a fiesta to thank the outreach team and to celebrate the homecoming of many who had grown up in this town and gone on to make their lives elsewhere. Isabella had been a bundle of excitement all day as she looked forward to her uncle Lucas's arrival. When Marley and the Tech women finished getting ready and made their way to the big party tent set up on the schoolyard, Isabella ran to greet them, dragging Lucas Montero along with her.

"Miss Marley, Miss Marley! He's here!" Isabella beamed up at the handsome, dark-haired man.

"Hi, Lucas. It's great to see you again." Offering a welcoming smile, Marley moved her camera strap to the opposite shoulder and extended her hand.

Lucas returned her firm grip. With his free hand he tugged on his niece's braid. "Izzy sure is happy to have you visit again. Ever since I got here this afternoon, it's been 'Marley this' and 'Marley that.'"

"I think Isabella's pretty special, too. Hey, let me get a picture of you two." She popped the lens cap of her camera and dropped to one knee in front of Lucas and his niece to snap a photo. Rising, she glanced over her shoulder and noticed the interested looks brightening the faces of the college coeds. They couldn't seem to tear their gazes away from the hunky Latino. Suppressing a knowing smile, she made the introductions. Then, leaving Lucas to deal with his admirers, she excused herself to capture a few candid photos before everyone sat down to eat.

As she made her way through the party tent, she glimpsed Ben surrounded by several laughing women. He spooned something from a dish Conchita Montero handed him, then howled and fanned his mouth with his ball cap. "Whoa, that's hot!"

Marley couldn't resist joining the laughter as she stepped closer and snapped several pictures. "Never underestimate Conchita's habaneros. Guaranteed to blister your taste buds faster than a blowtorch."

"Now you tell me." Ben's eyes watered like faucets. He crammed a folded tortilla into his mouth and collapsed onto the nearest picnic bench.

Conchita shook her head. "I warned this gringo who thinks he knows chili peppers."

While Ben frantically chewed and swallowed, Marley fetched a cup of ice water. She suppressed another chuckle as she handed him the cup and eased onto the bench beside him. "Better yet?"

"Some." His voice came out in a pained rasp.

He sipped more water. "I suppose you think I deserved this."

"I've heard you brag more than once about liking your Tex-Mex as hot as you can get it."

"I take it all back. Conchita's habaneros are the undisputed winner."

Marley reviewed the last few photos she'd taken, pausing at the one of Ben seconds after he'd sampled Conchita's salsa. "This one is definitely enlargement-worthy. I need to find a special place for it in my studio."

Leaning over for a look, Ben groaned. "I'll pay you good money to delete that right now. If my friends back in Houston ever see it, my reputation is history."

"Mmm, now I definitely have something to blackmail you with."

"You wouldn't—"

Marley grinned as she shut off the camera and moved it out of Ben's reach. At least things seemed more relaxed between them again.

Then his hand grazed hers, and electricity zinged through her. He cradled her fingers in his palm with such tenderness that she couldn't draw a breath. "Marley," he whispered as she gazed at their entwined hands. "I know I've done a lot of stuff wrong since we got here. But I've learned a lot, too. I wouldn't have missed this for anything. Especially..."

Slowly, she lifted her eyes to meet his. "Especially what?"

"Especially sharing it with you."

Marley blinked and looked away. Beyond the party tent, the pathways were lit with the golden glow of luminarias, votive candles nestled in sand inside brown paper bags. A similar glow spread through her chest, an uncanny mixture of fear and expectancy, and she sent up a prayer that if Ben fit into God's plan for her future, He'd open all the right doors to make it happen.

Ben awoke Wednesday morning to the usual symphony of snores from his RV mates. Today was different, though. He hadn't expected the rush of bittersweet nostalgia over his last sunrise in Candelaria. Last night's fiesta had been a fitting close to the trip, with good food, festive music and lots of presents for the children.

And Marley.

He squeezed his eyes shut, remembering how beautiful she looked in the candlelight.

As he crawled from the bunk, he dressed quickly and quietly so as not to disturb the others, then slipped out the door and into the pale pink blush of morning. Maybe he only imagined it, but somehow God seemed nearer in Candelaria. Nearer and more...compassionate. Forgiving. Real.

Ben ambled down the road toward the far end of town, the sun at his back and his long, thin shadow stretching out before him. As dawn painted the desert in hues of gold and peach against a sky growing bluer by the minute, Ben tilted his head and searched the heavens. "God, I'm sorry," he began, his throat aching. "I don't want to be a cynic any longer. I want to know You again, to trust You like I—"

The words clotted on his tongue. *Like I used to. Like when Mom was alive and my world wasn't collapsing around my feet.*

Out of nowhere, a verse from Scripture bloomed in Ben's thoughts: *"In this world you will have trouble. But take heart! I have overcome the world."*

His chest constricted as he relived the moment he'd last heard those words, read by the pastor at his mother's funeral. They'd sounded trite, a poor and unsatisfying explanation for everything wrong in the world.

But maybe everything wasn't supposed to make sense, at least this side of heaven. More than ever, Ben needed to believe God really was in control, even when parents died, jobs disappeared and families struggled to subsist in a ghost town.

"Ben? Are you okay?" Marley's gentle whisper sounded behind him.

Hauling in a deep breath, he composed himself, then slowly turned and smiled. "Just enjoying the sunrise."

"Coffee's on." A shadow of concern darkened her eyes. She poked her hands into the pockets of her hoodie. "We're having a quick breakfast of juice and cereal so we can finish loading and head home."

"Great. Be there in a sec."

With a lift of one brow, Marley glanced back over her shoulder. "Sure you're okay?"

Ben started to nod, then clamped his jaws together and shrugged. "Like I said last night, this experience has taught me a lot, mostly about myself. Guess I'm still processing it all."

"I felt the same the first time I came here." Marley gazed into the distance as her lips curled in a wistful smile. "It's like I tried to tell you. No one ever leaves Candelaria without being changed in some way."

"I believe it. Never thought I could care so much about the lives of perfect strangers."

"Except they aren't strangers anymore, are they?" She sighed, her gaze sweeping the sleepy little town.

"Marley, I—" No, he wasn't ready to peel away any more layers quite yet. He motioned toward the RVs. "Save me some breakfast, okay? I'll be along soon."

* * *

By nine o'clock, the team had the pickup and RVs packed and ready to go. Several families came out to say goodbye, including Conchita Montero, and Ben found himself wrapped in the woman's ample arms.

"*Muchas gracias*, Ben. Be good to our Marley, *sí?*" Conchita tweaked his chin. "I think you will have many years of happiness together."

Heat rose in Ben's cheeks. He glanced around to make sure Marley hadn't overheard. She was passing out hugs to several dark-haired children, saving the biggest and best for Isabella. With a sheepish grin, he faced Conchita. "So you don't think I'm such a cynic anymore?"

"No. *Dios* has answered my prayers for you."

Ben eyed her with a doubtful grimace. "How can you be so sure?"

"*Mi corazón sabe lo que es cierto.*" She patted her chest just above her heart.

Ben's Spanish might be rusty but he understood the gesture. Conchita's truth came from a place deep inside. He took her hands and squeezed them. "Keep praying for me, will you?"

She nodded and blew him a kiss as she stepped away.

Before long, the caravan headed up the long stretch of highway, leaving Candelaria little

more than a shimmering mirage behind them...
and leaving Ben with memories he hoped would
stay with him forever. He glanced over at Marley, behind the wheel of Ernie's pickup and
looking as relaxed and content as he'd ever seen
her. Clearly, these few days in Candelaria would
linger in her spirit for a long time to come.

He swallowed and shifted his gaze to the barren landscape speeding past his window. There
was no more denying he could easily fall in
love with the woman next to him. But why now,
when he was one job offer away from packing
his bags and hightailing it back to the city?

Is that what you really want?

A high-rise office overlooking crowded free-
ways? A posh but sterile condo that was little more than a place to crash at the end of a
twelve-hour workday? Getting his exercise on
treadmills in a mirrored room filled with dozens of other sweating bodies?

And leaving Marley behind?

For Marley, settling into quiet introspection
on the long drive back to Alpine was all part of
the Candelaria experience. She'd expected Ben
wouldn't talk as much as on the ride down, but
his utter silence worried her. She still savored
the closeness they'd regained at the fiesta last
night. Then this morning when she'd found him

before breakfast, he seemed on the verge of telling her something important.

Like maybe goodbye?

As they neared Marfa, Ben seemed to come out of his trance. With a breathy sigh, he shifted and pulled his cell phone from his pocket and stared briefly at the screen before tapping some buttons. Phone to his ear, he glanced toward Marley. "Just letting Uncle Steve know where we are."

She smiled and nodded, then returned her attention to the highway while Ben gave his uncle their approximate arrival time. After disconnecting the call, he laid the phone facedown on his thigh, then lifted it as if about to make another call or check an app, then abruptly shoved the phone back into his pocket.

"Not enough bars?" Marley kept her tone light.

"Signal's fine. Just changed my mind."

Another forty minutes of silence ensued as they drove on to Alpine. Arriving in the Spirit Fellowship parking lot, Marley recognized Steve Whitlow's white pickup and pulled up alongside. Shutting off the engine, she turned to Ben. "Why don't you head on home with your uncle? With the college kids, we have plenty of help to unload."

"Are you sure? Because it's no problem..."

One look in his eyes and she could see how ready he was to take her up on her offer. "I'm sure. Go home, kick back and decompress. That's what I plan to do as soon as we're done here."

"Thanks." Ben pushed open his door and set one foot on the pavement, then paused and turned. "I mean this, Marley. Whatever comes next, I'll never forget these past three months."

Whatever comes next. Not exactly the words her heart wanted to hear, but she nodded silently and stepped from the pickup. After Ben retrieved his duffel from behind the seat, they strode over to where Ernie and Pastor Chris were talking to Steve Whitlow, apparently making arrangements to clean up the RV inside and out before returning it to him.

"No hurry," Steve said. "Jane and I don't have travel plans until spring." He grinned as Marley and Ben drew near. "Heard y'all had another successful mission trip."

"Ben was a great addition to the team." Marley glanced at Ben's drooping shoulders. "I think we wore him out, though."

Following his uncle to the pickup, Ben offered a tired wave that was little more than the twitch of two fingers. A few seconds later they drove away, and the end-of-trip emptiness in the pit of Marley's stomach deepened even more.

Pitching in with unloading gear and seeing off the college students on their way back to Lubbock distracted her for another couple of hours, but by the time she made it home to her apartment, she barely had the energy to drop her luggage by the door, grab a soda from the fridge and collapse on the sofa.

She'd just dozed off when her cell phone chimed. With a groan, she forced herself upright and snatched the phone from her purse on the coffee table. As soon as she recognized the Missouri area code, she almost pressed the ignore button.

Then, guilt nagging, she answered. "Mom?"

Chapter Thirteen

"No, this is your father."

Marley sat up straight, dread tightening her stomach. "Is Mom okay?"

"She's fine, except for trying to reach you several times over the last few days and worrying herself sick." The slight echo to the phone connection made him sound even more cold and distant. "I'm surprised you even care."

"Of course I care. I've been out of town, with no cell service." A headache spread behind Marley's eyes. "She knew I was going on another mission trip."

Her father grew silent. When he spoke again, exasperation laced his tone. "You're a businesswoman, Marsha. You need to take your responsibilities more seriously."

"I take them plenty seriously. But these mission trips are important to me, and—" She would *not* have this conversation with him. "Anyway, I'm back now."

"Just so you don't expect me to bail you out when you can't pay next month's rent."

She cringed, remembering the looming rent increase. "I'll be fine, Dad." *Somehow.*

"Good, glad to hear it." The edge to her father's voice eased slightly. "Marsha—Marley—you know your mother and I only want what's best for you."

"I know. I appreciate everything you've done to help me get established here, and I hope one day I can repay you. But I need you to trust me to manage my business my way."

"Even when you're clearly making foolish decisions?"

Marley closed her eyes and took a steadying breath. "You can't have it both ways. You wanted your delinquent daughter out of your life, so I left Missouri and changed my name. It's about time you gave up trying to control every little thing I do."

"That isn't fair—"

"I'm hanging up now, Dad. Give Mom my love and tell her I'll call after I catch up on some rest." She turned off her cell and tossed it onto the coffee table.

The headache had grown to monstrous proportions. Marley dug through her purse again for a travel-size bottle of ibuprofen and downed two caplets with the remains of her cola. Flopping back on the sofa cushions, she covered her eyes with one arm and prayed for sleep to take away the pain.

But now, as she replayed the conversation with her father, sleep wouldn't come. Naturally, he believed his financial investment earned him a say in how she ran her photography business. All the more reason she must make it on her own and find a way to pay him back. She was good, and she knew it. Ben had a point—with the right connections and in a larger city, she could do so much better than small-town portrait photography and the occasional magazine assignment. If she could prove herself successful in her own right, maybe her father would no longer be embarrassed to claim her.

Then reality hit. Sitting up, Marley cradled her head in her hands and recalled all those short-lived promises her father had once made about being a better parent. After Marley's arrest for shoplifting, then a confrontation in the church parking lot with Pastor Henke and Healy Ferguson, Mom had finally coerced Marley's father into attending parenting classes. For a while, they all thought Harold Sanderson truly wanted to change.

They couldn't have been more wrong. As he'd

done for as long as Marley could remember, he found it too easy to blame everyone else for his problems. And the old Marsha Sanderson had slipped right back into her rebellious ways.

Thank goodness Pastor Henke and the Fergusons hadn't given up on her, or she might be rotting in a Missouri jail today, never knowing the peace and hope God's forgiveness could bring. To this day, though, she regretted the lost opportunity to ask for Tina Maxwell's forgiveness after the accident, but with Tina's lengthy rehab and Marley's journey through the juvenile legal system, they never saw each other again. The next thing Marley knew, Dad had arranged her new identity and relocation to Alpine, and here she intended to stay.

No, she didn't need fame or recognition or wealth. She'd earned the respect of the local business community, and she had friends who loved her for the person she'd become. Her simple life in Alpine was as good as it got.

After twelve straight hours of sleep, Ben felt almost human again. He hadn't realized how physically exhausted he was until Uncle Steve had to shake him awake just to get him in the house after their drive back to the ranch. Aunt Jane practically force-fed him the meatloaf and mashed potatoes she'd fixed for supper, saying he'd sleep better on a full stomach. Then he'd hauled himself to bed and drifted off before the sun went down.

After a shower and shave, Ben wandered into the kitchen, where he found Aunt Jane at the table with a mug of coffee and the morning paper.

She looked up with a gleam in her eye. "Look who the cat dragged in. Can I fix you some breakfast?"

"I can manage." With a sleepy grin, he took a box of wheat flakes from the cupboard, poured himself a bowl and added a splash of milk. He filled a coffee mug, then carried his breakfast to the table.

Aunt Jane allowed him about two minutes before she peppered him with questions about the mission trip. She wanted to know which projects he worked on, if he met Conchita's new baby grandson, what he thought of the college students from Tech, if he thought he'd ever go back.

Laughing tiredly, he dropped his spoon and held up both hands. "I haven't been home a full day yet. Give me time to let it all sink in!"

Aunt Jane's eyes narrowed as she cast him a knowing smile. "You called this *home*."

"Don't get any ideas. It was only a figure of speech." Ben scooped up another bite of wheat flakes. While he'd been answering her questions, his cereal had grown soggy. He swallowed with a grimace. "I can't keep freeloading off you forever. I need to find a job, even if it's flipping burgers somewhere."

He was only half-kidding. After his call to Uncle Steve during the drive back yesterday, he'd decided to put off checking email for responses to his résumés. For one reason, he hadn't wanted to risk disappointment. For another...a positive reply might mean saying goodbye to Marley and any chance they had that their friendship could lead to something more.

Carrying her mug to the sink, Aunt Jane glanced over her shoulder, a sympathetic tilt to her brows. "Steve and I prayed about you the whole time you were away. God knows exactly where He wants you, and it's going to be a thousand times better than you ever imagined for yourself."

"I hope you're right." Ben rose and set his dishes in the sink, then kissed his aunt on the cheek. "In the meantime, I have some things I need to take care of in town."

"If you're worried I'm gonna fuss at you for burying your nose in those internet job sites—"

"God *does* want me to be proactive, don't you think?" At Aunt Jane's sharp glance, he continued, "All right, I admit it. I'd really like to see Marley again."

Eyes wide and sparkling, Aunt Jane squeezed his hand. "You give her a big ol' hug from me, okay?"

Oh, he'd like to. Nothing he'd enjoy more.

An hour later, he parked in front of Marley's studio, glad to see the Open sign in the window in spite of the ladders and scaffolding. Men in paint-spattered coveralls worked overhead, well along on the refurbishing project.

As he stepped from the Mustang, he glimpsed Marley bustling about inside the studio. Less than twenty-four hours had passed since he'd last seen her, but already it felt like a lifetime. A smart man wouldn't even be here, knowing how slim their chances were. Yet here he was, and if the jumpy feeling in his belly was any indication, he was about to get a lot stupider.

When Marley saw him through the window, she paused. A look of surprise quirked her brows. Then she smiled and pulled open the door. "Hey, stranger. What brings you back to town so soon?"

He didn't have a good answer—at least none he could easily voice—so he merely shrugged and meandered inside. His glance took in a couple of new framed prints on the wall. "You took these in Candelaria. I recognize the sunset."

"After these trips, I can't wait to go through my photos. It's like opening presents." Marley stood beside him and studied the picture. "I love this shot, but it doesn't begin to compare with the real thing."

Just like Ben's thoughts of Marley when they were apart didn't compare to the reality of being with her. He inched closer, his hand brushing hers. An odd smile twisted her mouth as she slid her gaze toward him.

His mouth went dry. "Marley, this thing between us...believe me, I'm in no hurry for it to end, but..."

"I get it. Your career comes first." Her forced smile didn't hide the hurt behind her eyes. Or the hope. She moved behind the counter and continued her unnecessary straightening. "Don't apologize, Ben. I've had fun getting to know you these past few months, and it was great having you on the Candelaria trip. But this isn't your home—"

That word again: *home.*

"—and as soon as the holidays are over, I'm sure the perfect job offer will come through, and you can get on with your life." Marley tossed a pencil into the drawer and slammed it shut— harder than she intended, judging by the startled look on her face.

Ben rested his elbows on the counter, his

gaze searching Marley's. "What if I'm starting to hope that day never comes?"

She sucked in a tiny breath. "What are you saying, Ben?"

"I'm saying it's getting harder and harder to think about leaving Alpine. Leaving *you*." His jaw clenched. He swiveled his head to stare out the front window and recalled the day he'd seen the young family pass by on the sidewalk. "I've had my life planned out since college. Launch my career, climb the corporate ladder, establish myself as an indispensable member of the team." He released a harsh laugh. "Then I found out exactly how dispensable I am."

"Ben…" Marley reached for his hand.

"I'm not looking for sympathy, just trying to sort everything out." Without releasing her hand, he moved around the counter until they stood toe-to-toe. With his other hand, he cradled her cheek. "What I'm trying to say is, I never in a million years planned to care this much for you."

Marley froze. She couldn't make her lungs work if she tried. Ben's palm against her cheek felt hot and cold at the same time.

Eyelids pressed shut, she somehow forced movement into her limbs and took a shaky step backward. When Ben's hand fell away from her face, it felt as if he'd stolen a part of her. She turned away with a silent sigh. "Please...don't."

"Don't what? Don't admit the truth?" Ben's voice had grown husky. "If I learned anything from everything I've experienced lately, it's that I need to be honest with myself, and with the people I care about."

Marley dared a glance, though the look in his eyes nearly undid her. "Even when we both know it's hopeless? I'm here in Alpine. You'll soon be going...who knows where."

"Can't you take pictures anywhere? Why does it have to be Alpine?"

There he went, tempting her again with possibilities she knew in her heart would never be right for her. "You're not getting it. I love it here. I have my friends, my church, my business..." She shook her head as if he could never understand. "My *life*."

Ben's jaw muscles bunched. "Guess I misread the signals. For a while there, I thought maybe you were starting to feel something for me."

Leaning against the counter, Marley rested her head in her hands. The tiny gold swirls in the white Formica countertop swam before her eyes. "You didn't misread anything."

Two solid arms wrapped around her, drawing her upright. Ben touched his forehead to hers, and she breathed in the musky scent of his aftershave. "Then give us a chance," he murmured. "The other thing I learned in Candelaria—I guess I should say *re*learned—is what it means to have faith. For the first time in a long time, I've been praying. And I have a real hard time believing God would bring you into my life if He didn't have a plan to keep us together."

Fresh tremors of hope surged through Marley—hope for a future she never imagined could be hers. The love of a good man. Someone with whom she could finally and fully share every part of herself, even the past she'd kept private for so long.

When Ben slid his hand behind her head and lowered his mouth to hers, it felt like the most natural thing in the world.

It also felt like leaping off a cliff and seeing the ground rushing toward her with no way to stop the fall. Because there was nothing to be done but to give herself over to the rush of emotions. She melted into Ben's tender kiss as her arms encircled his torso.

"Ahem."

Only then did the jangle of bells over the front door penetrate Marley's consciousness. Looking past Ben's shoulder, she glimpsed Janet Harders, her friend from the antiques shop next door.

Marley edged out of Ben's embrace and plucked at the hem of her blouse. As she pasted on a nervous smile, she hoped her cheeks weren't as red as they felt. "Hi, Janet. What can I do for you?"

The dark-haired woman pushed the door closed behind her. "I was hoping to go over some details about this weekend." Janet would be hosting a family reunion over Christmas and had arranged for Marley to photograph the group. Her smile tilted playfully. "But if this is a bad time…"

"Not at all. Ben and I were just…um…" Tugging at her mussed ponytail, Marley looked to Ben for help, but with arms crossed and head down, he seemed intent on staying out of it. In fact, she was certain she heard him quietly snickering. Marley motioned her friend toward the table in the corner. "Have a seat and I'll be right with you."

As Janet made herself comfortable in one of the chairs, Marley returned her attention to Ben, who had sobered somewhat, thank goodness. She didn't need to be any more rattled than she already was. "I'll be busy for a while. But we should talk. We could have lunch later."

"Good idea." Ben grazed her cheek with a quick kiss. "I'll be back in an hour."

As he headed toward the door, Marley could hardly tear her eyes away. Just before he stepped outside, he shot her a lazy grin that sent ripples through her abdomen. By the time she retrieved the Harders file from her office and sat down beside Janet, she'd required more than a few steadying breaths.

With the paperwork spread between them, Marley assumed her most professional tone. "Now, what did you want to discuss about the reunion?"

At the coffee shop down the street, Ben couldn't resist checking email to see if his résumés had garnered any responses. Not that he expected anything a week before Christmas, but there they were—not one but *two* interview opportunities.

Ben's head reeled. One was for an advertising manager's position at a textile company in some town he'd never heard of in Wisconsin. Yeah, he could not see himself shoveling snow in January. Besides, the salary range was significantly lower than what he'd earned at his previous job.

The second opening was only slightly more appealing but would require relocating to Seattle. Living clear across the country would make it a lot harder to mend the ties with his family in Houston.

He sipped a cappuccino and stared at his laptop screen while he debated how to respond.

Considering these were among the few viable job leads he'd had so far, didn't he owe it to himself to at least make the interviews? Both had said they could do the preliminaries over Skype. He wouldn't have to worry about the expense of plane fare unless he made it to the next level.

Just pray about it.

The thought soothed his churning brain like a cool summer rain on parched grass. For the past few years, he'd done little enough praying about his future. Instead, he'd simply charged ahead on his own terms and expected success.

How's that been working for you? he could almost hear God saying.

He set down his coffee cup and folded his hands under the edge of the table. For all anyone else knew, he was merely deep in thought. Focused on the toes of his sneakers, now several shades grimier that when he bought them, he settled in for a long overdue heart-to-heart with his Maker.

True, he'd dipped his toes in the river of prayer a few times in Candelaria, but the idea of immersing himself in the full power of God made him want to grab for the nearest lifeline. When would he get it into his head that God *was* his lifeline, and the only one worth holding on to?

His mom had understood this. She lived out

her faith every day. But maybe that explained why her sudden death had shattered his own fragile faith. How could you trust a God who allowed an undiagnosed heart problem to take the life of a woman loved and needed by so many?

He knew what his mother would say: "No matter how bad life gets, God never, ever abandons us." She'd have told him to look for God's fingerprints in both joy and heartache, because every experience, good or bad, had a beautiful and important life lesson wrapped inside.

Mom's death, Dad's remarriage, Ben's job loss.

These months in Alpine, meeting Marley, joining the Candelaria outreach.

For I know the plans I have for you...

A long, slow sigh seeped from Ben's lungs as he raised his head and sat up. Waking his computer, he typed quick replies to both interview requests. Though he had misgivings about either job being right for him, he stated his availability for a Skype appointment within the next few days. He'd leave the final decision up to the Lord.

He'd just shut down his computer when his cell phone vibrated. Marley's name appeared on the caller ID. As he answered, a smile crept into his tone. "Hey. I was just on my way back to the studio."

"Good. I'm starved. Where do you want to go for lunch?"

They decided on a sandwich shop a couple of blocks from Marley's studio. Ben swung by to pick her up, arriving as she stepped onto the sidewalk and locked the front door.

She climbed into the passenger seat and moaned appreciatively as she sank into the leather upholstery. "A girl could get seriously attached to this car."

"So now the truth comes out. It's my Mustang you're really interested in." Ben revved the engine before pulling into the street. After baring their feelings earlier, he sensed they were both working hard to keep things light. "How'd your meeting go?"

"Fine. Janet brought a list of family members so I could start planning how to group them for photos." Marley twisted the strap of her shoulder bag. "Were you at the coffee shop checking email?"

"Uh, yeah."

"And?"

Ben pulled the Mustang into a parking spot across from the sandwich shop and shut off the engine. "How about we talk about it after lunch?"

"Tell me now, okay?" She stared straight

ahead. "I won't be able to eat a bite if I'm wondering where things stand."

Ben took Marley's hand, tugging gently until she looked at him. Confusion and doubt filled her gaze, and he knew he had to find a way to bring back the hope he'd seen there this morning.

"I need you to trust me on this," he said, stroking the back of her hand. "More than that, we both have to trust God. Spending time with you has reminded me how important faith is."

With a shudder, Marley brushed a tear from her cheek. "Crazy, isn't it? You're finding your faith again, and I'm struggling with mine." She freed her hand and clawed through her purse until she found a tissue. "All these years on my own, I had no option but to trust God. Suddenly I'm terrified He'll say no to the one thing I want most."

"Does it help at all to know I want the same thing, too?" She nodded, and he tweaked her chin. "Then let's give God a chance to work out the details. Whaddya say?"

Chapter Fourteen

After lunch, Ben dropped Marley back at the studio, and she fairly floated through the rest of the afternoon. Maybe she was living in a dream-world, but the longer it took Ben to find new employment, the more hopeful she became that he might stick around permanently. He seemed content to stay in Alpine with his aunt and uncle for the time being, but he'd been too successful in his former career to settle for just anything.

Money must be getting tight, though, because after her comment about getting attached to his Mustang, he'd casually mentioned over lunch that it might be time to sell it. He joked about trading those hungry "420 horses" under the hood for a single horse fueled by oats and hay, but Marley could tell he didn't relish the idea of parting with his shiny red status symbol. And she couldn't picture her hunky city boy driving anything else.

Finishing up in the darkroom, Marley hung her apron on a hook and returned to the showroom. Any minute now, a potential client would arrive to discuss a photo shoot for the grand opening of a new restaurant in town, along with other professional images for promoting the business. Hoping to impress the restaurateur, Marley had already gathered appropriate samples of her work along with price lists. If the meeting went well, the income could keep Marley in her studio for another month or two without having to go to her father for help.

As she arranged her materials on the corner table, her studio phone rang. She checked the caller ID—unknown. Possibly Mom, but she didn't usually call the studio number unless Marley wasn't picking up her cell. Either way, Marley didn't have the energy or the time to talk her mother through another bout of despondency over her life as a politician's wife.

Hesitantly, she pressed the talk button. "Good morning. Photography by Marley Sanders."

"Is this Miss Sanderson?" The unfamiliar male voice made her stomach clench. "Marsha Sanderson, from Aileen, Missouri?"

"Who is this?"

"I take it I've found the right person. And

I must say, you haven't changed much in ten years." She could have sworn the man stifled a triumphant laugh. "I could hardly believe it when I came across your picture in a newspaper this week. Congratulations on your new life, Marsha."

"You're mistaken. There's no one here by that name." Trembling, Marley disconnected the call.

Who had tracked her down? Was she supposed to do nothing while this reporter or private eye or whoever he was exposed her as Representative Harold Sanderson's delinquent daughter? Dad would be furious!

Maybe the man would listen to reason. Somehow, she had to make him understand it was in everyone's best interests not to reveal her real name. Intending to call him back, she checked the recent call list, then groaned as she remembered he'd called from an unlisted number.

This couldn't be happening, not now! Should she call Dad, or just wait and see if the caller did anything with his discovery?

The restaurateur's arrival removed her choices. "Miss Sanders, nice to finally meet you in person."

"You, too, Mr. Hillman." Marley extended her hand, only to realize how badly it shook.

Embarrassed, she forced a smile and invited the man to have a seat at the corner table.

The meeting went badly. Distracted by her worries, Marley couldn't seem to put a coherent thought together. An hour later, when she saw Mr. Hillman out, she guessed from his noncommittal "Thanks, I'll be in touch," that she'd probably lost the chance to serve his photography needs.

At least she hadn't heard from her anonymous caller again. *Please, Lord, let him just drop it!*

On the other hand, if the man did intend to make trouble, Marley should at least give her father some warning. In the office, she retrieved her cell phone from her purse, but before she could dial her father's number, the phone rang in her hand and she nearly clawed the ceiling. Seeing Ben's name on the caller ID, she breathed a sigh of relief, only to start shaking again as she envisioned trying to explain to him about her real identity. If there was any chance at all of something real between them, he deserved to know the truth, but she wanted to tell him on her terms, not because some scandalmonger forced her hand.

She tried to disguise the tremor in her voice. "Hi, Ben."

"Hello, Marley. Or should I call you Marsha?"

* * *

Ben gripped his cell phone as if clinging to his last ounce of trust while he waited for Marley to say something—*anything*—to convince him he hadn't fallen in love with a lie.

"Ben, we need to talk." Her voice quavered. He could barely hear her. "But not like this. Meet me at my place. I'll explain everything."

He stared out the kitchen window, oblivious to Aunt Jane hovering nearby. "Just answer me. Are you really an ex-delinquent from Missouri named Marsha Sanderson?"

Silence stretched between them, until she murmured, "Yes."

"That's all I need to know." Ben jammed the end button with his thumb and let his arm drop to his side. Still, he didn't move from the window.

Aunt Jane rested her hand on his shoulder. "So it's true?"

"Guess so."

"Oh, Ben…" His aunt guided him to a chair and made him sit down. Good thing, because all the strength seemed to have drained from his knees. "Surely she had good reasons for keeping this a secret. Didn't you give her a chance to explain?"

"What's to explain? She lied to me. She lied to all of us."

Uncle Steve marched into the kitchen. "Just got off the phone with Neil Ingram from the *Avalanche*. The same guy called him early this morning digging for information. Neil's as stunned as we are."

Aunt Jane sat across from Ben. "Son, this doesn't change the person Marley is. She's obviously done her best to put the past behind her and start over."

"Maybe so, but..." Ben lurched to his feet and paced across the kitchen. "As much as we've shared the past few months, I can't believe she didn't respect me enough to tell me the truth."

"Now hold on, son. You're not being fair." Ben's uncle cornered him in front of the refrigerator. "Ever since you rolled into Alpine, you've held the possibility of your next job over all our heads, especially Marley's. You expect her to risk confiding her deepest secrets when any day now you could leave her high and dry?"

"It's not like that. Wherever I end up, I was ready to ask her to come with me. But now?" Ben wrapped his arms against his sides. "I feel like I don't even know her anymore."

"You know her just fine," Aunt Jane said, coming to stand on his other side. "You know everything about her that matters."

A tiny part of him knew his aunt was right. Anyone who cared as much about helping others as Marley did must have a good heart, whatever she'd done in her past. But to be blindsided with this kind of news, just when he'd let himself imagine a real future with Marley, left the fragile fabric of his trust—his *faith*—in tatters. It felt like God had let him down again.

Lowering his head, he released a long, pained breath. "I need space so I can figure this all out. I'm going home to Houston."

Uncle Steve's mouth firmed. "At least talk to Marley first."

"I can't, not until I get my head together. Maybe after Christmas…"

His aunt and uncle shared a look, disappointment clearly reflected in Aunt Jane's eyes. She'd already decorated the tree and filled several cookie tins with goodies. Just this morning, she'd suggested that since Marley didn't have any family around, Ben should invite her to spend Christmas with them.

Except now he knew Marley *did* have a family. Her father was a rich and influential state representative in the Missouri legislature. Confusion swept over him again. *Why, Marley? Why all the secrets?*

Taking a step back, Ben lifted both hands defensively. "Look, you've both been after me to mend fences with my dad and Paula. If I spend Christmas in Houston, maybe it'll give us time to work on it. As for everything else…" He shook his head. "Like I said, I need time to think."

Edging past his aunt and uncle, he marched to the guest room to pack. Ten minutes later, he aimed his Mustang for the highway. Barring traffic problems, in eight or nine hours he could be sleeping in his own condo again.

Marley tugged another tissue from the box under the counter and blew her nose. Too distraught to think about work, she closed the studio and phoned Pastor Chris at the church office. "I need to talk. Can I come over?"

"You've been crying, Marley. I hear it in your voice. What happened?"

"I'll tell you when I get there. And…would you ask if Ernie and Angela can meet us? This is going to be hard enough. I'd rather not have to repeat everything for them."

Worry laced the pastor's tone. "This sounds serious. Give me half an hour to clear my schedule, then I'm here for whatever you need."

By the time Marley composed herself enough to make the drive to Spirit Fellowship, Angela and Ernie were already waiting for her in the pastor's office.

Angela gestured for Marley to take the center chair, between her and Ernie. She reached over to squeeze Marley's arm. "It's okay, honey. Whatever this is about, we're here for you."

Pastor Chris joined them a few moments later. "Katherine's holding my calls," he said as the door clicked shut. He circled to his desk chair, then folded his hands and sat forward with a worried frown. "What's going on, Marley?"

Plucking a tissue from her purse, she dried a fresh spurt of tears. "Remember the El Paso newspaper Ben brought back from Presidio?"

"Yes, of course. It was great publicity for Spirit Outreach."

"I hope you still think so after what I have to tell you." This was the worst of it, the possibility of her painful past casting a pall over the good their outreach committee was doing.

Doubtful glances passed between Pastor Chris and the Coutus, while Marley braced herself to explain. "Someone recognized me in the newspaper photo. I don't know who it is yet, or what he plans to do next, but there could be trouble."

Pastor Chris's frown deepened, but the sheen of concern never left his eyes. "What kind of trouble are we talking about, Marley?"

Her only hope was to cling to God's forgiveness and trust Him to see her through this. Even if Ben or her friends here in Alpine never forgave her for holding back the truth, she refused to be ashamed of the person she was today.

She sat a little straighter, her voice strengthening. "I'm not who you think I am. My real name is Marsha Sanderson, and my father is Missouri State Representative Harold Sanderson. For the past decade, I've been living under an assumed identity because my father's PR team worried my juvenile offender record would reflect badly on his political career."

Utter silence blanketed the small office as her friends took in her revelation. Finally Pastor Chris said softly, "And this changes things how?"

She met his gaze and read forgiveness and understanding in his eyes. With a grim sigh, she answered, "I seriously doubt the man who found me has any intention of sitting on this information. Once the news gets out, you should be prepared for the media to descend. And it won't be pretty."

The pastor rounded the desk and propped one hip on the edge. "Reporters, I can handle. However, I *am* worried about you. How can we help?"

His kindness brought another rush of tears, and Angela shoved more tissues into her hand. When she could speak again, she murmured, "Just be my friends."

Ernie clamped a hand on her shoulder. "That's a given. We don't care who you used to be, and I'll personally thrash anyone who dares to dis Marley Sanders."

Marley laughed in spite of herself, amazed that they hadn't even asked what horrible things she'd done as a teen. "You have no idea what your support means to me. But...are you sure this isn't going to be a problem for the church? For the outreach ministry?"

Tapping a finger to his chin, Pastor Chris nodded thoughtfully. "I think our best approach is to face this head-on. Marley, I'd like you to share your story in an open letter to the congregation. In your own words, let them know how the Lord has worked in your life, healed and forgiven you, and brought you into His service. Then, when those pesky reporters show up, you'll have the whole family of Spirit Fellowship standing beside you."

His words made sense. Even more freeing was the relief of having her identity and her past out in the open. No more living in dread of discovery. No more worrying about the effect on her father's reputation. *That*, she would find out soon enough. And the truth was, she didn't care. Only one thing mattered now—convincing Ben to give her a chance to explain.

Until then, she'd get started on the letter to

her church family. Declining Angela's invitation to spend the rest of the day with her, Marley drove straight home. She'd turned off her phone before leaving for the meeting with Pastor Chris and was almost afraid to turn it back on. After Ben had hung up on her this morning, she'd immediately found three missed calls, all anonymous. Probably the same person who'd tracked her down at the studio had also somehow obtained her cell number. Naturally, he didn't leave messages.

But what if Ben had tried to call again? She plopped on the sofa and stared at the black display, then prayed as she pressed the on button. A whole string of anonymous calls appeared, intermixed with several from the number her mother had last used.

Nothing from Ben.

Nothing she could do about it, either. If he wasn't ready to talk, she wouldn't force him. In the meantime, she'd better get the call to her parents over with. Drawing a long, slow breath, she pressed the redial button.

"Marsha?" Her father answered, his voice full of rage. "Do you have any idea of the damage you've done? Getting your photograph spread all over Texas, leaving yourself open to be recognized—what were you thinking?"

"You should have expected something like

this to happen sooner or later." Marley did her best to sound calm and mature, but inside, she was still a little girl aching for her father's approval. "Daddy, I'm doing good now, making a difference with my life. Can't you just be proud of me?"

"Proud of you? When—" A scuffling sound interrupted him, then muted voices.

Marley's mother came on the line. "Honey, we *are* proud of you." To Marley's amazement, Mom sounded strong, positive, in control. "This will all work out for the best—I don't care what your father says. Let me handle him, okay?"

"Mom—"

"I'm serious. This foolishness has gone on long enough. Now, I have some other calls to make, but I'll be in touch very soon. I love you, sweetie." The line went dead.

Stunned, Marley dropped the phone into her lap. Could this really signify a change in her relationship with her parents? She'd hoped before, only to be disappointed. But back then, she hadn't understood the power of prayer.

Maybe this time things would be different.

Ben wanted things to be different. On so many levels. He wanted Mom to be alive. He wanted his old job back. He wanted to reclaim some semblance of security instead of won-

dering when the next major disappointment
would hit.

On Thursday night, finding nothing to eat in
his condo except a box of graham crackers and
a nearly empty jar of peanut butter, Ben went to
bed hungry. The next morning, he grabbed coffee and a stale cinnamon roll at a convenience
store, then drove around until his annoyance
with Houston traffic made him wonder why he
ever thought he liked city life.

When his stomach told him it was lunchtime,
he decided to check out a popular restaurant on
Westheimer where the Home Tech managers
often ate on Fridays. Couldn't hurt to put out
some feelers in case the company was hiring
again. But when he glimpsed a former under-
ling in deep conversation with the media mogul
Ben had courted for months, he quietly slipped
out to his car.

Did he need further convincing he hadn't
been indispensable?

The idea of hanging out in his lonely condo
didn't appeal, so Ben drove over to his brother's
and spent the afternoon entertaining Aidan's
twin toddlers, freeing Aidan's wife, Renée, to
run some errands.

By the time Aidan arrived home from work,
Ben had turned the twins over to their mom
and was chilling out on the patio with a cold

drink. Aidan loosened his tie as he plopped down in the chair next to Ben's. "Couldn't believe it when Renée called to say you were back in town. Does this mean you got a job?"

"I wish." Ben swirled the melting ice slowly diluting his soda. "Nope, just needed to get out of Alpine."

"But you love it out there with Uncle Steve and Aunt Jane." Aidan shot him a teasing grin. "Anyway, I heard you were getting sweet on a certain young lady photographer."

"Didn't work out." Ben had tried all day not to think about Marley. Leave it to his brother to remind him.

Aidan studied him. "This isn't only about losing your job or Dad remarrying, is it? What else is going on?"

"It's Marley, the girl I've been seeing. Everyone's always assumed she's this honest, hardworking, mission-minded Christian girl."

"And you found out she *isn't* all those things?"

"No. I mean, she is…now." Ben raked his fingers through his hair as if the action would clear the tangle of doubts from his brain.

With a confused grimace, Aidan shook his head. "I think you'd better back up and tell me the whole story."

Ben described the strange phone call he'd gotten early yesterday, when he'd learned Marley was really the daughter of a Missouri state representative. Before he could finish, Renée peeked out the door. "Honey, the boys are getting wild. Can you keep them occupied while I get dinner ready?"

Aidan shot Ben an apologetic smile. "You can tell me the rest later. Want to help with the kids?"

"Yeah, be right there." Ben stood and picked up his glass, but as he turned toward the door, the new-email chime sounded on his phone. Still hoping for a job lead, he couldn't afford to ignore it.

The message came from Uncle Steve, and the subject line read: FWD: FWD: To my brothers and sisters at Spirit Fellowship. The email, originally sent at 2:43 p.m. yesterday, first went to Pastor Chris Arndt, who'd forwarded it to Uncle Steve, who'd forwarded it to Ben.

And the sender was Marley Sanders.

All breath leaving his lungs, Ben collapsed into the chair. What was this—excuses, another cover-up? Still, he couldn't resist reading on.

The email began with a short message from his uncle:

Ben, I pray you'll read this with an open mind. Whatever happened in Marley's past, don't doubt her sincerity. I know she loves you, and I know you love her.

The last part was true, anyway. Otherwise, Ben wouldn't hurt nearly this much.

Steeling himself, he scrolled down to where Marley's message began. She explained how, at the urging of her father's campaign managers, she'd legally changed her name and left her former life behind. She described her past as a juvenile offender—shoplifting, underage drinking, traffic violations and finally a terrible accident that nearly killed the friend who'd continually tried to talk Marley down from her out-of-control behavior.

Thanks to a reformed ex-con and his wife in Marley's hometown of Aileen, Missouri, Marley eventually confronted her mistakes and resolved to make amends. When her father strongly suggested she "disappear" and start over somewhere else in a place where no one knew anything about her or the horrible things she'd done, it seemed like a God-given opportunity to turn her life around. She'd chosen to attend college at Sul Ross, mainly because Big Bend Country seemed so remote that no one from her past or her father's political connections would likely ever cross her path.

Then she'd fallen in love with Alpine and her

new church family at Spirit Fellowship. The out-reach to Candelaria had shown her a way to give back, to somehow begin to atone for all her mistakes. But the truth is, she wrote, I've never had to earn God's forgiveness, because He forgave me even before I asked, and the Bible assures me my name is written in heaven.

Ben read the email twice more, and each time his regret multiplied tenfold. What kind of idiot was he, letting doubts and questions mar his judgment? How could he turn his back on the best thing that had ever happened to him? The day he first stepped inside Marley's studio, some small part of him must have already known his life was about to change. Everything about Marley attracted him—her beauty, her talent, her unshakable faith.

Maybe it was her faith most of all, because until he started spending time with Marley, he hadn't realized how much he'd missed his relationship with the Lord.

But right now, he really, really missed Marley.

The side gate creaked, and Ben glanced up to see his dad and Paula step onto the patio. Rising, he clicked off his phone and stuffed it in his pocket. "Hey, Dad."

In three strides, his father wrapped him in a bear hug. "What are you doing here, son? Not that I'm sorry to see you, but I thought you were spending Christmas in Alpine."

"Long story." Ben didn't have the energy to go into it again. When his dad released him, he made himself smile and nod at Paula. She was no more deserving of his judgment than Marley, and it was high time he made peace with his father's remarriage.

Paula's hesitant smile warmed slightly. "Are you back to stay?"

"Actually, I'm headed back to Alpine tomorrow." Ben hadn't even known his own plans until the words popped out of his mouth, but he knew he had to return. Whatever his future held, it would begin with asking Marley's forgiveness and praying she'd give him another chance.

Chapter Fifteen

Marley spent most of Saturday afternoon photographing the Harders family reunion. She couldn't thank Janet enough for her compassionate response to Marley's open letter. In fact, everyone in town so far had been extremely kind and understanding.

Even so, the thought of facing all that sympathy at church Sunday morning was a wee bit intimidating. Instead, Marley decided to take this one Sunday off to worship and pray in the solitude of her apartment.

After some Scripture reading, prayer and a second cup of coffee, she settled onto the sofa to reread Neil Ingram's article in the *Avalanche*. In a follow-up to the pieces he'd written about Spirit Outreach's ministry to Candelaria, he promised to put a positive spin on the big reveal about Marley's former life, and she had to admit he'd done an excellent job. He'd even re-printed excerpts from the email she'd sent to the Spirit Fellowship congregation.

Apparently, Dad's staff had already begun damage control. In a statement released late Friday, Harold Sanderson declared he couldn't be prouder of his daughter. "Everyone deserves a second chance," he was quoted as saying, "and if those who have held the highest office in the country can rise above ignominy, surely my constituents will be no less forgiving of a young woman who clearly has made every effort to turn her life around and become a contributing member of society."

Naturally, Marley's father had yet to direct such sentiments to her personally, not that she expected him to. It would be a long time before he forgave her for forcing him into this corner.

Mom, on the other hand, had already telephoned several times, each time sounding happier than Marley had heard her in years. "You know what this means, don't you?" Mom had said after Dad made his official public statement. "You can come home where you belong, maybe even for Christmas! You can even change your name back to Marsha."

"Sorry, Mom. I've been Marley Sanders for too long. This is who I am now, and Alpine is my home." She agreed she might return to Missouri for a visit soon, but it wouldn't be this Christmas.

At the sound of her doorbell, Marley laid the *Avalanche* aside. It wasn't even noon yet, and on a Sunday morning she certainly wasn't expecting any visitors. *Please, Lord, not some nosy reporter who's found out where I live.*

It turned out to be the very *last* person she'd expected to see on her doorstep: Ben.

"Hi, Marley." He stood on the small porch, the fingertips of both hands jammed in his jeans pockets. "I took a chance you'd be here this morning, or else you'd have come home to find me camped on your doorstep. Are you still speaking to me?"

She raised a brow. "Depends on what you have to say."

"How about I start with 'I'm sorry'?"

"An apology is usually a good place to start." Beneath his tan windbreaker, Marley noticed the maroon T-shirt, one she'd helped him shop for the first day they met. The slim fit accentuated his solid chest, all the more developed since he'd been working on the ranch with his uncle.

The special times they'd shared—organizing the fund-raiser, horseback riding together, the trip to Candelaria—brought a clutch to her throat. She turned away.

Ben reached for her hand. "Please, Marley. Give me another chance."

"I heard you went home to Houston." She kept her eyes averted. "Why did you come back?"

"Because leaving was the worst mistake I ever made." He pulled her around to face him. "I was wrong, Marley. I let my own insecurities cast doubts on what we have together. Please say you forgive me."

She slid her hands free and hugged them to her ribs as she swiveled away. She had a comfortable life here, friends who accepted her, a ministry she cared deeply about, and—despite the current financial worries—a fulfilling career. If she let Ben back into her life, would she only be risking more heartache?

His arms snaked around her from behind, his chin resting on her shoulder and his breath warm upon her cheek. "I'm crazy about you, Marley." Yearning tinged his tone. "I'll do anything—be anything—if you'll just give me another chance."

"Oh, Ben…" With a sad-eyed smile, she turned to face him and pressed her hand to his cheek. "I don't want you changing for me. If I've learned anything from all this, it's that we have to be true to ourselves. Most of all, to God."

"But I've already changed. *You* changed me." Ben drew her closer, one hand working through her hair and loosening her ponytail. "Marley... I love you so much." His searching gaze settled on her mouth before he lowered his lips to hers.

A languid warmth filled her as she returned his kiss. She wanted this. All these years, she'd avoided relationships for fear of the truth coming out...until Ben came along. He'd burrowed into her heart with his city-boy charm, then showed her again and again how thoroughly he embraced the things she cared about most.

Tasting the salt of her own tears, she clasped her hands behind his neck and nestled her face into the cleft of his shoulder. "I love you, too, Ben—more than I ever imagined I could love anyone."

"Then let's see this through, okay?" One finger under her chin, he lifted her head and smiled into her eyes. "We can make this work, Marley. I know we can."

She wanted to say yes, to trust that somehow they really could have a future together. "I'm scared." *Scared of losing you all over again.* "You needed time to think. Now, so do I. These last few days have turned my world upside down."

"I understand." He stepped back, dropping his hands to his sides. "Look, it's still several days till Christmas, and maybe by then we'll both have clearer heads." His tone grew timorous. "Would you consider coming out to the ranch? Because I'd really love to spend Christmas with you."

Marley squeezed her eyes shut at the sudden sharp pain beneath her heart. "I can't, Ben. I'm spending Christmas with Ernie and Angela."

"Okay." He nodded, his gaze shifting sideways before he fixed her with a pleading look. "But maybe you could come out later in the day and have some eggnog and cookies with us. If not for me, then for Uncle Steve and Aunt Jane? They think the world of you, and it would mean a lot to them."

With a tired sigh, Marley rested her hand on the doorknob, a silent signal to Ben that he needed to leave. "I'll think about it. That's all I can promise."

"Well, I tried." Ben plopped onto the sofa in the Whitlows' great room. The nine-foot spruce by the front windows mocked him with its cheery lights and the Christmas angel smiling down from the top branch.

"Oh, Ben." Aunt Jane looked up from her knitting. "Poor thing's been through so much lately. She probably just needs time to sort through it all."

He sat forward, the heels of his hands pressed into his eye sockets. "I've really messed things up, haven't I? There's got to be a way to make Marley believe how sorry I am, how badly I want to be with her."

Uncle Steve's boots clopped across the hardwood floor and Ben raised his head. His uncle sank onto the other end of the sofa. "Are you about ready to talk turkey about your future? Because the way I see it, until you settle on what you're going to do with your life—more importantly, *where*—Marley isn't likely to take any more chances on you."

Ben glared at his uncle. "I get it. Totally. But I haven't had one single job offer I'd seriously consider."

"Not even working right here on the ranch with me?"

"I love it here, you know I do." A frustrated growl tore from Ben's throat. "But I'm not a rancher. All my experience is in corporate management."

Uncle Steve glanced over at Aunt Jane, and she nodded. Shifting to reach into his back pocket, Uncle Steve tugged out a business card and handed it to Ben. "Then this could be your answer, a chance to have the best of both worlds."

Ben looked at the card: Dean Radcliffe, Executive Director, Big Bend Assistance Alliance. "I remember he came out the day of the trail ride. Pastor Chris and Marley were talking to him about outreach ministry support."

Aunt Jane laid aside her knitting and reached across to squeeze Ben's arm. "Mr. Radcliffe spoke to our adult Sunday school class this morning. He's moving ahead with plans to open a branch office right here in Alpine, and he's looking for an administrator. I didn't want to say anything and get your hopes up—or ours, either—but while you were out this afternoon, I took the liberty of emailing Mr. Radcliffe your résumé." Her smile widened. "He emailed back not twenty minutes later to say he's very impressed. He wants you to give him a call tomorrow."

The twinge of anticipation zinging through Ben's abdomen easily eclipsed any irritation he felt over his aunt's presumptuousness. He turned to Uncle Steve. "But…you said the best of both worlds. What did you mean?"

"I mean my offer to partner with me on the ranch is still open. Honestly, Ben, your kind of business sense and promotional experience would be a huge asset. And what you don't know about horses and cattle ranching, I can teach you, because someday…" Uncle Steve's throat bobbed, his eyes misting over.

"What he's trying to say," Aunt Jane began softly, "is that since we don't have kids of our own, we'd like the ranch to be yours someday."

Now Ben was getting choked up. He looked from one to the other as he contemplated the real possibility of spending the rest of his life right here in Alpine.

Right here at the ranch.

But even with a real job prospect—no, make that *two* opportunities offering both personal fulfillment and the chance to help others—his life wouldn't be complete without one very important addition. Somehow, he had to convince Marley they could have a future together, that he'd never let her down again.

The twinkling Christmas tree lights reminded him of a special evening in Candelaria, and the germ of an idea began to form. But in order for it to work, he had to make sure Marley came out to the ranch for Christmas.

He shoved up from the sofa. "I need to make a trip to town."

"But you just came from town," Aunt Jane said. "What's so important that it can't wait till tomorrow?"

The rest of my life, he wanted to shout. "I'm working on a plan. I'll tell you about it after I get a few more details figured out."

Ben headed directly to the Coutus' house, hoping he could catch them both at home on a Sunday evening.

Ernie answered the door, his flat-lipped scowl clearly expressing his current opinion of Ben. "Didn't know you were back in town."

"Leaving was a mistake. I don't plan to make any more."

"Does Marley know you're back?"

"I saw her earlier today." Ben looked away briefly. "That's why I'm here. I need your help with something."

"If you want me to convince her to give you another chance, you're wasting your time." Retreating a step, Ernie prepared to shut the door in Ben's face.

"Please, give me ten minutes. Then if you still want to throw me out, you can."

By now, Angela stood at Ernie's shoulder. She tugged on his arm. "Ernie, invite him in. Marley's right, sometimes you're entirely too judgmental for someone who calls himself a Christian."

With a dramatic sigh, Ernie stepped aside and waved Ben through the door. "Ten minutes. I'm starting the countdown now."

Ben followed Angela to the living room, where Christmas carols played on the stereo. While Ernie turned down the music, Angela took a seat on the sofa across from the chair she offered Ben. Ernie remained standing, arms folded.

Ben got right to the point. "I'm in love with

Marley, and I need to convince her I'll be here for her, no matter what. Yes, it hurt when I found out about her past, but it was more about *how* I found out, and I'm sorry for my stupid, selfish response."

Ernie snorted. His wife shot him a chiding glance.

Rubbing perspiring hands on his jeans, Ben quickly described his hopes for staying and working right here in Alpine. "But now I've got to make Marley believe it's possible, and that's where you come in."

"What is it you want us to do?" Angela asked.

"I know Marley plans to spend Christmas Day with you, but I've also invited her out to the ranch later. Could you please give her a nudge in that direction? I'm planning something special that I hope will show her exactly how I feel about her."

Lips pursed, Ernie fixed Ben with a knifelike stare. "So help me, Fisher, if you hurt Marley again—"

"Honey…" Angela's dulcet tone didn't match the glare in her narrowed eyes. She turned to Ben. "Naturally, we can't force Marley to go to the ranch if she doesn't want to, but it might help if you clued us in on what exactly your plan involves."

Ben closed his eyes briefly and pictured the

scene he had in mind. "I still have a few things to figure out. But you might pray for a clear evening and no wind."

With a quick glance at Ernie, Angela nodded. "All right, then, we'll do whatever we can to help."

"Thank you." Ben stood. "Just one more thing. Please don't tell her I came to see you. I need this to be a surprise."

He left the Coutus' feeling only slightly more hopeful. Angela was right—if Marley decided she didn't want anything more to do with Ben, there was no way they'd convince her to drive out to the Whitlows' on Christmas Day.

His faith was really getting a workout lately, stretching and growing him in ways he'd never expected. Now he'd have to trust the Lord about his future with Marley.

He spent the next couple of days putting his surprise together, beginning first thing Monday with a trip to the hardware store. On Monday afternoon, he had a telephone interview with Dean Radcliffe, and by Tuesday he'd been offered the administrative position for the new Alpine branch of Big Bend Assistance Alliance. Salary-wise, it meant a huge step down for Ben, but at this point the money didn't matter. Now that he had also agreed to work with his uncle managing the ranch, his big-city expenses were a thing of the past.

He might hold on to his Mustang, though, if for no other reason than he knew how much Marley enjoyed riding around in it.

Christmas week at the studio left Marley searching for anything to keep busy. Janet came over on Tuesday morning to look through the proofs from the family reunion. Afterward, they talked over coffee about how the building renovations were coming along.

"So you think you'll stay awhile?" Janet asked. "I know you've been worried about covering the higher rent."

"It's still iffy, but my mother sent me enough to get me through the next couple of months." Marley stifled a sardonic laugh. After her past came out, Dad's public display of support was tempered with his private declaration that since neither of them had anything more to hide, Marley was perfectly free to sink or swim on her own. Mom's hefty check arrived shortly thereafter.

The solution was only a temporary one, though, because Marley had no intention of continuing to rely on Sanderson money. She'd already come up with one possibility for generating more income. After reading Neil Ingram's article in Sunday's paper, the school superintendent had come by to see Marley yesterday. He felt she had a lot to offer as a mentor for high-risk kids and wanted to get her involved with a program at the high school. In conjunction with the program, he hoped to get the school board to fund a part-time teaching position for a photography class.

Marley could easily see how photography could be a way to reach kids on the edge, but until now, she'd never considered herself mentor material, partly because she hadn't been free to be open about her own mistakes.

She didn't say any more to Janet about her talk with the superintendent, but as soon as Janet returned next door to her antique shop, Marley decided to telephone Healy and Valerie Ferguson back in her hometown of Aileen.

"Do it," Healy said. "I know your outreach ministry means a lot to you, and you're doing good work there. But when you see troubled teens finding their way back from disastrous choices, you *know* you've made a lasting difference."

Valerie, listening on speakerphone, heartily agreed. Her tone grew teary as she said, "Do you know how proud we are of you, Marley Sanders?"

The use of her chosen name was like a blessing, an assurance that this new life she'd been given was truly God's gift. Like Jacob became Israel. Like Saul became Paul. Marley reached for a tissue to dry her own eyes. "I thank God every day for sending both of you into my life."

After a pause, Valerie said, "Honey, is there something else?"

Leave it to Valerie, who always could read between the lines. "I'm falling in love with someone, but I'm scared it'll never work between us."

Healy's breathy chuckle sounded through the phone line. "I know that feeling. And I also know God can work anything out, if it's meant to be."

"Trust your heart," Valerie said. "We'll be praying for you."

Ending the call, Marley said a prayer of her own for God's direction, because where Ben was concerned, she didn't feel at all confident in the direction of her own heart.

Chapter Sixteen

On Christmas Day afternoon, Marley propped her feet up on the Coutus' coffee table and groaned. She really shouldn't have eaten a third slice of Ernie's mother's pumpkin cheesecake. A sugar high definitely wasn't conducive to clear thinking, and she still hadn't decided whether to accept Ben's invitation to drive out to the Whitlow ranch later. Strangely, Ernie and Angela kept dropping not-so-subtle hints that Marley should think about paying a call on the Whitlows. Did they even know Ben had returned to Alpine?

As Ben's image filled her thoughts, the last serving of cheesecake sat even heavier. When Ernie's dad came through with the coffeepot, she waved him away. Maybe she should just go home to her apartment. She'd promised her mother a long phone call later, and with the whole Marsha/Marley news beginning to settle down, she'd begun to have hope of developing a better relationship with her parents. Dad might never be the father she needed him to be, but then it wasn't up to Marley to fix him. All she could do was keep praying.

A sad smile crept across her lips as she imagined family Christmases again, she and her siblings and their spouses and kids gathered for the holidays with their parents. Seemed like forever ago since the last time they were all together.

Before her thoughts grew any more maudlin, Marley decided to take her leave. Finding Angela in the kitchen, she thanked her for a wonderful day.

"Oh, so you're heading out to the Whitlows' now?"

She frowned. "I don't think that's such a good idea."

Angela seized Marley's hand and practically dragged her into the walk-in pantry. "Okay, I wasn't supposed to say anything, but I'm going to anyway. Marley, you *need* to go see the Whitlows."

Cleary, something was up. Marley's gaze sharpened. "You've been bugging me about this all day. What do you know that I don't?"

Arms crossed, Angela glared right back. "I know that if you don't go, you'll regret it the rest of your life." Her look turned pleading. "Ben loves you, Marley. Don't give up on him too soon."

Angela and Ernie taking up Ben's cause? Marley couldn't believe it. "Has he talked to you?"

"Does it matter? Just *go*." Gripping Marley by the shoulders, Angela steered her to the entryway closet and helped her on with her jacket. Practically shoving her out the front door, she called, "And don't forget to call me later and tell me all about it!"

Ben stared out the front window. To the southwest, a pale winter sun crept lower, soon to be swallowed by the distant mountains. "She's not coming."

"Don't give up yet." Aunt Jane slid one arm around his waist and pressed her cheek against his shoulder. "You wanted it nearly dark for your surprise."

"It won't be much of a surprise without the guest of honor." With a resigned groan, Ben stepped away from the window. "I'll tell Uncle Steve we can unsaddle—"

"Wait, is that a car?" Aunt Jane squinted and leaned closer to the glass.

Ben was afraid to look. Afraid to be disappointed.

"It is. Ben, it's Marley!" His aunt bounced on her toes like an excited six-year-old.

Ben yanked her sideways. "Don't let her see us."

"Oh, pshaw. Afraid she'll think you've been wearing a trench in my floor from all your pacing?"

And he probably had. "I just don't want to look too anxious and make her even more uncomfortable."

"Mmm-hmm." With a smug smile, Aunt Jane edged toward the kitchen. "I'll just let Steve know to be ready."

Mouth dry, stomach in knots, Ben peeked around the curtain as Marley's Honda pulled up in the circle drive. Feet planted firmly in place, he took several steadying breaths to keep from racing to the door before she had a chance to make it up the porch steps.

After she rang the bell, he sent up one more quick prayer before inviting her in. "You made it."

"Yeah." Marley entered hesitantly. She glanced around the room as if expecting monsters to pop out from behind the furniture.

Aunt Jane bustled in from the kitchen. "Marley, how wonderful to see you!" She wrapped Marley in a warm hug. "Merry Christmas, honey! Here, let me take your coat—"

Behind Marley, Ben made a slicing motion across his throat.

The whites of Aunt Jane's eyes flashed. She stepped back. "On second thought, keep your coat on. You and Ben should go take a walk and watch the evening stars come out. Looks like it's going to be a beautiful night."

"That's okay." Marley shot Ben an uneasy glance. "I just wanted to come out and wish you and Steve a merry Christmas. I can't stay long."

"Well, you have time for a walk." Aunt Jane draped an arm around Marley's shoulders and aimed her toward the kitchen. "Anyway, Steve's out...doing something, and won't be in right away."

Ben appreciated his aunt's help, but her enthusiasm was a wee bit over the top. If she didn't take it down a notch, she'd raise Marley's suspicions even higher than they probably already were.

He'd conveniently left his own jacket on a kitchen chair and grabbed it on their way through. On the back porch, he paused and took Marley's hand. "Thank you for coming. I wasn't sure you would."

"I almost didn't." She pointedly withdrew her

hand and tucked it into her pocket. "What exactly is going on here, Ben? Ernie and Angela were acting weird all day, and now your aunt is skipping around like the cat who ate the canary. After the complicated week I've had, I don't think I can handle any more surprises."

Ben ducked his head and grinned shyly. "I promise you won't be disappointed."

Disappointment wasn't what Marley feared most. What really scared her was the rebellious pounding of her own pulse just being this close to Ben again. All right, she'd go along for this sunset walk Jane Whitlow insisted they take. Deep-breathing the chilly night air might be exactly what she needed to kick-start the willpower required to hold her heart in check.

But why were they strolling toward the barn? Better question, why were Dancer and Skeeter saddled, bridled and clipped to the cross ties? The gentle gray lifted his sleepy head and nickered as Marley neared.

Scratching Dancer's nose, Marley shot Ben an accusing stare. "This is no coincidence, is it?"

He grinned back, taking in her jeans and sneakers. "I'm just glad you didn't show up in a dress and heels, or I'd have had to spill eggnog on you so you'd have to borrow riding clothes from Aunt Jane."

"Dress and heels—*me*?" She'd laugh if this weren't such an impossible situation. Instead, she sucked in her cheeks in an indignant frown. "Mighty sure of yourself, aren't you?"

The smile left his face. "Not in the least."

She studied him for several long moments, then tore her gaze away and began unclipping Dancer from the cross ties. She hoped Ben couldn't see her hands shaking. "Obviously, you planned for us to go riding. So let's get it over with."

Without a word, Ben boosted her into the saddle. While she settled her feet in the stirrups— conveniently adjusted to her correct length, she couldn't help noticing—Ben unclipped Skeeter and swung himself up with the grace of a seasoned cowboy.

Before he noticed her watching him, she drew a quick breath and faced forward. Ben took the lead on the Palomino, and Marley noticed they followed the same route they'd used for the trail ride. As the sky turned from orange to deep purple and the first stars popped out overhead, a nervous tingle crept up her spine. "Is it safe to be out riding this late? What about snakes or wild animals or—"

"Don't worry, Marley. We'll stay on the trail, and we won't go far." Ben's back swayed in a loose rhythm with Skeeter's motion. "Anyway,

I've got flashlights in the saddlebags if we need them."

"Of course you do," Marley muttered under her breath. She gripped the pommel a little tighter.

Shortly after they passed through the first gate, Marley spotted Steve Whitlow riding toward them on a stocky horse that looked almost black in the waning light. He called a greeting. "Nice night for a ride. Y'all have fun."

Interesting. Steve didn't stop, and neither he nor Ben mentioned a word about whatever the "something" was that Jane said he'd gone out to take care of.

Yes, this was definitely a setup. If Marley weren't so curious now to find out exactly what this scheme of theirs involved, she'd turn around right now and go home.

To your lonely, empty apartment? Even her skittishness over a cross-country horseback ride in the dark with the man who could turn her dreams to dust wasn't enough to make that choice appealing.

It's Christmas, Marley. Have a little faith.

When Ben glanced back at her from several yards ahead, she realized she'd reined Dancer almost to a crawl. Or maybe the horse had sensed her uncertainty and slowed to allow her time to collect her courage. Either way, this indecision couldn't last, because her aching heart couldn't take the strain. She had two choices: end things with Ben once and for all, or give their love a chance.

No, she really needed to give God a chance, to let Him show her what He could do with two hearts entwined with His.

Two hearts...she must be seeing things, because they'd just reached the ridge where Jane and Steve had brought her to see the wildflowers last fall. A shimmer of light rose up from where the land fell away beyond the ridge. As Dancer moved closer and Marley peered into the rolling valley below, she glimpsed dozens of luminarias, their golden glow outlining the shape of intertwined hearts.

She let go of the pommel and covered her mouth to stifle a gasp. "Oh, Ben..."

In a tiny, timid voice, he murmured, "Surprise!"

She couldn't speak, couldn't even swallow over the lump in her throat. She hardly noticed when Ben climbed down from Skeeter and then helped Marley to the ground. Her teary gaze riveted to the scene in the valley below, she nestled deep into Ben's embrace.

His lips grazed her temple. "Please tell me those are happy tears."

She nodded, searching his face and seeing

the love in his eyes. "I can't believe you did this for me."

"I would do anything for you, Marley. Don't you get it? I'm crazy in love with you."

The same old doubts threatened to strangle the hope she felt. "But your career. What happens to us if—"

He silenced her with a finger to her lips. "Are you ready to trust what we have and leave the future in God's hands?"

The right answer was yes, but Marley couldn't dredge up the courage to speak it. What if God said no to this dream? What if He took Ben a thousand miles away and—

"Marley." Ben's tone grew insistent. Gently, he swiveled her to face him straight on, his arms locked firmly around her waist. "If I can learn to stop co-opting God's plan for my life—for *our* lives—and trust Him to work things out, can't you?"

This time, the answer came easily. "Yes."

"Then believe this. I love you, and I'm never leaving you again." Releasing her, he eased a step away and reached for something inside his jacket pocket. "And just to prove it…"

She froze. "Ben, what are you doing?"

"Now, don't panic." He grinned his adorable boyish grin. "This isn't a ring—yet—but it'll have to serve as my pledge until we get that little detail taken care of." His hand reappeared with a folded sheet of white paper. "This is an email I got a couple of days ago. Take a look."

The quickly fading amber streaks from the setting sun offered barely enough light to read the message, but Marley quickly got the gist of it. Dean Radcliffe of Big Bend Assistance Alliance had offered Ben the administrative position for the new Alpine branch.

Mouth agape, she looked up at him, searching for confirmation.

"I'm staying in Alpine, Marley." His gaze remained steady, his eyes full of promise. "And if you need more proof, I'm sure I can get my uncle to sign a paper confirming I'm going into business with him here on the ranch."

Now she really couldn't believe what she was hearing. "You. You're going to be a rancher?"

Ben laughed softly. "That remains to be seen. But I did agree to take over some of the management responsibilities while Uncle Steve works on teaching me the rest." He pulled her close again. "Do you hear me? Your city boy isn't going anywhere. I'll be around for as long as you'll have me, and I hope it's the rest of our lives."

His words finally penetrated, soaking deep inside Marley's heart. While candlelight flick-

ered and her hopes soared on the most beautiful Christmas she'd ever known, she tipped her
head to welcome Ben's kiss.

* * * * *

Dear Reader,

When my friend suggested I write a story about Candelaria, Texas, I was intrigued. As I learned more about this tiny border town and the deeply ingrained family values of the people there, ideas began to percolate. I'd always wanted to revisit the characters from one of my earlier novels, and I realized Marley was exactly the heroine I needed for this story—a woman with a painful past in search of atonement and forgiveness.

But the truth is, we never have to earn forgiveness from God. Jesus paid for our sins on the cross, and there is nothing more we need to do except believe. That isn't to say we shouldn't strive to help others like Marley did, but our good deeds become acts of gratitude for the forgiveness that is already ours through Christ.

Another theme of this story is trusting God's plan. It's more than just "Let go and let God," though. Ben had to learn the difference between forging ahead on his own and being humbly proactive in a way that gave God plenty of room to work out His purposes.

Thank you for joining me on Marley and Ben's journey. I love to hear from readers, so please contact me through my website, www.MyraJohnson.com, or write to me c/o Love Inspired Books, Harlequin Enterprises, 233 Broadway, Suite 1001, New York, NY 10279.

With blessings and gratitude,
Myra

LARGER-PRINT BOOKS!

GET 2 FREE
LARGER-PRINT NOVELS
PLUS 2 FREE
MYSTERY GIFTS

Love Inspired
SUSPENSE
RIVETING INSPIRATIONAL ROMANCE

Larger-print novels are now available...

REQUEST YOUR FREE BOOKS!
2 FREE WHOLESOME ROMANCE NOVELS
IN LARGER PRINT
PLUS 2
FREE
MYSTERY GIFTS

✻✻✻✻✻✻✻✻✻✻✻✻✻✻✻✻✻✻✻✻✻✻✻✻

HEARTWARMING™

✻✻✻✻✻✻✻✻✻✻✻✻✻✻✻✻✻✻✻✻✻✻✻✻

Wholesome, tender romances

READERSERVICE.COM

Manage your account online!

- Review your order history
- Manage your payments
- Update your address

> *We've designed the*
> *Reader Service website*
> *just for you.*

Enjoy all the features!

- Discover new series available to you, and read excerpts from any series.
- Respond to mailings and special monthly offers.
- Connect with favorite authors at the blog.
- Browse the Bonus Bucks catalog and online-only exculsives.
- Share your feedback.

Visit us at:
ReaderService.com